BOOKS BY ALAN SILLITOE

*Love in the Environs of Voronezh
and Other Poems (1969)*

Tree on Fire (1968)

The Death of William Posters (1965)

Road to Volgograd (1964)

*The Ragman's Daughter and
Other Stories (1964)*

Key to the Door (1962)

The General (1961)

*The Loneliness of the
Long-distance Runner (1960)*

Saturday Night and Sunday Morning (1959)

THE
LONELINESS
OF THE
LONG-DISTANCE
RUNNER

❧❧❧❧❧

THE
LONELINESS
OF THE
LONG-DISTANCE
RUNNER

by *Alan Sillitoe*

NEW YORK   ALFRED · A · KNOPF

19 *75*

Contents

THE
LONELINESS
OF THE
LONG-DISTANCE
RUNNER

The Loneliness of the Long-distance Runner

AS soon as I got to Borstal they made me a long-distance cross-country runner. I suppose they thought I was just the build for it because I was long and skinny for my age (and still am) and in any case I didn't mind it much, to tell you the truth, because running had always been made much of in our family, especially running away from the police. I've always been a good runner, quick and with a big stride as well, the only trouble being that no matter how fast I run, and I did a very fair lick even though I do say so myself, it didn't stop me getting caught by the cops after that bakery job.

You might think it a bit rare, having long-distance cross-country runners in Borstal, thinking that the first thing a long-distance cross-country runner would do when they set him loose at them fields and woods would be to run as far away from the place as he could get on a bellyful of Borstal slumgullion—but you're wrong, and I'll tell you why. The first thing is that them bastards over us aren't as daft as they most of the time look, and for another thing I'm not so daft as I would look if I tried to make a break for it on my long-distance running, because to abscond and then get caught is nothing but a mug's game, and I'm not falling for it. Cunning is what counts in this life, and even that you've got to use in the slyest way you can; I'm telling you straight: they're cunning, and I'm cunning. If only 'them' and 'us' had the

same ideas we'd get on like a house on fire, but they don't see
eye to eye with us and we don't see eye to eye with them, so
that's how it stands and how it will always stand. The one
fact is that all of us are cunning, and because of this there's
no love lost between us. So the thing is that they know I won't
try to get away from them: they sit there like spiders in that
crumbly manor house, perched like jumped-up jackdaws on
the roof, watching out over the drives and fields like German
generals from the tops of tanks. And even when I jog-trot on
behind a wood and they can't see me anymore they know my
sweeping-brush head will bob along that hedge-top in an
hour's time and that I'll report to the bloke on the gate.
Because when on a raw and frosty morning I get up at five
o'clock and stand shivering my belly off on the stone floor and
all the rest still have another hour to snooze before the bells
go, I slink downstairs through all the corridors to the big outside door with a permit running-card in my fist, I feel like the
first and last man on the world, both at once, if you can
believe what I'm trying to say. I feel like the first man because
I've hardly got a stitch on and am sent against the frozen
fields in a shimmy and shorts—even the first poor bastard
dropped on to the earth in midwinter knew how to make a
suit of leaves, or how to skin a pterodactyl for a topcoat. But
there I am, frozen stiff, with nothing to get me warm except
a couple of hours' long-distance running before breakfast, not
even a slice of bread-and-sheepdip. They're training me up
fine for the big sports day when all the pig-faced snotty-nosed
dukes and ladies—who can't add two and two together and
would mess themselves like loonies if they didn't have slavies
to beck-and-call—come and make speeches to us about sports
being just the thing to get us leading an honest life and keep
our itching finger-ends off them shop locks and safe handles

and hairgrips to open gas meters. They give us a bit of blue ribbon and a cup for a prize after we've shagged ourselves out running or jumping, like race horses, only we don't get so well looked-after as race horses, that's the only thing.

So there I am, standing in the doorway in shimmy and shorts, not even a dry crust in my guts, looking out at frosty flowers on the ground. I suppose you think this is enough to make me cry? Not likely. Just because I feel like the first bloke in the world wouldn't make me bawl. It makes me feel fifty times better than when I'm cooped up in that dormitory with three hundred others. No, it's sometimes when I stand there feeling like the *last* man in the world that I don't feel so good. I feel like the last man in the world because I think that all those three hundred sleepers behind me are dead. They sleep so well I think that every scruffy head's kicked the bucket in the night and I'm the only one left, and when I look out into the bushes and frozen ponds I have the feeling that it's going to get colder and colder until everything I can see, meaning my red arms as well, is going to be covered with a thousand miles of ice, all the earth, right up to the sky and over every bit of land and sea. So I try to kick this feeling out and act like I'm the first man on earth. And that makes me feel good, so as soon as I'm steamed up enough to get this feeling in me, I take a flying leap out of the doorway, and off I trot.

I'm in Essex. It's supposed to be a good Borstal, at least that's what the governor said to me when I got here from Nottingham. "We want to trust you while you are in this establishment," he said, smoothing out his newspaper with lily-white workless hands, while I read the big words upside down: *Daily Telegraph.* "If you play ball with us, we'll play ball with you." (Honest to God, you'd have thought it was

going to be one long tennis match.) " We want hard honest
work and we want good athletics," he said as well. " And if
you give us both these things you can be sure we'll do right
by you and send you back into the world an honest man."
Well, I could have died laughing, especially when straight
after this I hear the barking sergeant-major's voice calling me
and two others to attention and marching us off like we was
Grenadier Guards. And when the governor kept saying how
' we ' wanted you to do this, and ' we ' wanted you to do that,
I kept looking round for the other blokes, wondering how
many of them there was. Of course, I knew there were thousands of them, but as far as I knew only one was in the room.
And there *are* thousands of them, all over the poxeaten
country, in shops, offices, railway stations, cars, houses, pubs
—In-law blokes like you and them, all on the watch for Out-
law blokes like me and us—and waiting to 'phone for the
coppers as soon as we make a false move. And it'll always be
there, I'll tell you that now, because I haven't finished making
all my false moves yet, and I dare say I won't until I kick the
bucket. If the In-laws are hoping to stop me making false
moves they're wasting their time. They might as well stand
me up against a wall and let fly with a dozen rifles. That's the
only way they'll stop me, and a few million others. Because
I've been doing a lot of thinking since coming here. They can
spy on us all day to see if we're pulling our puddings and if
we're working good or doing our ' athletics ' but they can't
make an X-ray of our guts to find out what we're telling ourselves. I've been asking myself all sorts of questions, and
thinking about my life up to now. And I like doing all this.
It's a treat. It passes the time away and don't make Borstal
seem half so bad as the boys in our street used to say it was.
And this long-distance running lark is the best of all, because

it makes me think so good that I learn things even better than when I'm on my bed at night. And apart from that, what with thinking so much while I'm running I'm getting to be one of the best runners in the Borstal. I can go my five miles round better than anybody else I know.

So as soon as I tell myself I'm the first man ever to be dropped into the world, and as soon as I take that first flying leap out into the frosty grass of an early morning when even birds haven't the heart to whistle, I get to thinking, and that's what I like. I go my rounds in a dream, turning at lane or footpath corners without knowing I'm turning, leaping brooks without knowing they're there, and shouting good morning to the early cow-milker without seeing him. It's a treat, being a long-distance runner, out in the world by yourself with not a soul to make you bad-tempered or tell you what to do or that there's a shop to break and enter a bit back from the next street. Sometimes I think that I've never been so free as during that couple of hours when I'm trotting up the path out of the gates and turning by that bare-faced, big-bellied oak tree at the lane end. Everything's dead, but good, because it's dead before coming alive, not dead after being alive. That's how I look at it. Mind you, I often feel frozen stiff at first. I can't feel my hands or feet or flesh at all, like I'm a ghost who wouldn't know the earth was under him if he didn't see it now and again through the mist. But even though some people would call this frost-pain suffering if they wrote about it to their mams in a letter, I don't, because I know that in half an hour I'm going to be warm, that by the time I get to the main road and am turning on to the wheatfield footpath by the bus stop I'm going to feel as hot as a potbellied stove and as happy as a dog with a tin tail.

It's a good life, I'm saying to myself, if you don't give in to

coppers and Borstal-bosses and the rest of them bastard-faced
In-laws. Trot-trot-trot. Puff-puff-puff. Slap-slap-slap go my feet
on the hard soil. Swish-swish-swish as my arms and side catch
the bare branches of a bush. For I'm seventeen now, and
when they let me out of this—if I don't make a break and see
that things turn out otherwise—they'll try to get me in the
army, and what's the difference between the army and this
place I'm in now? They can't kid me, the bastards. I've seen
the barracks near where I live, and if there weren't swaddies
on guard outside with rifles you wouldn't know the difference
between their high walls and the place I'm in now. Even
though the swaddies come out at odd times a week for a pint
of ale, so what? Don't I come out three mornings a week on
my long-distance running, which is fifty times better than
boozing. When they first said that I was to do my long-
distance running without a guard pedalling beside me on a
bike I couldn't believe it; but they called it a progressive and
modern place, though they can't kid me because I know it's
just like any other Borstal, going by the stories I've heard,
except that they let me trot about like this. Borstal's Borstal
no matter what they do; but anyway I moaned about it being
a bit thick sending me out so early to run five miles on an
empty stomach, until they talked me round to thinking it
wasn't so bad—which I knew all the time—until they called
me a good sport and patted me on the back when I said I'd
do it and that I'd try to win them the Borstal Blue Ribbon
Prize Cup For Long Distance Cross Country Running (All
England). And now the governor talks to me when he comes
on his rounds, almost as he'd talk to his prize race horse, if he
had one.

" All right, Smith? " he asks.

" Yes, sir," I answer.

He flicks his grey moustache: "How's the running coming along?"

"I've set myself to trot round the grounds after dinner just to keep my hand in, sir," I tell him.

The pot-bellied pop-eyed bastard gets pleased at this: "Good show. I know you'll get us that cup," he says.

And I swear under my breath: "Like boggery, I will." No, I won't get them that cup, even though the stupid tash-twitching bastard has all his hopes in me. Because what does his barmy hope mean? I ask myself. Trot-trot-trot, slap-slap-slap, over the stream and into the wood where it's almost dark and frosty-dew twigs sting my legs. It don't mean a bloody thing to me, only to him, and it means as much to him as it would mean to me if I picked up the racing paper and put my bet on a hoss I didn't know, had never seen, and didn't care a sod if I ever did see. That's what it means to him. And I'll lose that race, because I'm not a race horse at all, and I'll let him know it when I'm about to get out—if I don't sling my hook even before the race. By Christ I will. I'm a human being and I've got thoughts and secrets and bloody life inside me that he doesn't know is there, and he'll never know what's there because he's stupid. I suppose you'll laugh at this, me saying the governor's a stupid bastard when I know hardly how to write and he can read and write and add-up like a professor. But what I say is true right enough. He's stupid, and I'm not, because I can see further into the likes of him than he can see into the likes of me. Admitted, we're both cunning, but I'm more cunning and I'll win in the end even if I die in gaol at eighty-two, because I'll have more fun and fire out of my life than he'll ever get out of his. He's read a thousand books I suppose, and for all I know he might even have written a few, but I know for a dead cert, as sure as I'm sitting here, that what I'm scribbling down is worth a million to what he could ever scribble down. I don't care what anybody says, but that's the truth and can't be denied. I know when he talks to me and I look into his army mug that I'm alive and he's dead. He's as dead as a doornail. If he ran ten yards he'd drop dead. If he got ten yards into what goes on in my guts he'd drop dead as well—with surprise. At the moment it's dead blokes like him as have the whip-hand over blokes like me, and I'm almost dead sure it'll always be like that, but even so, by Christ, I'd rather be like I am—always on the run and breaking into shops for a packet of fags and a jar of jam—than have the whip-hand over somebody else and be dead from the toe nails up. Maybe as soon as you get the whip-hand over somebody you do go dead. By God, to say that last sentence has needed a few hundred miles of long-distance running. I could no more have said that at first than I could have took a million-pound note from my back pocket. But it's true, you know, now I think of it again, and has always been true, and always will be true, and I'm surer of it every time I see the governor open that door and say Goodmorning lads.

As I run and see my smoky breath going out into the air as if I had ten cigars stuck in different parts of my body I think more on the little speech the governor made when I first came. Honesty. Be honest. I laughed so much one morning I went ten minutes down in my timing because I had to stop and get rid of the stitch in my side. The governor was so worried when I got back late that he sent me to the doctor's for an X-ray and heart check. Be honest. It's like saying: Be dead, like me, and then you'll have no more pain of leaving your nice slummy house for Borstal or prison. Be honest and settle down in a cosy six pounds a week job. Well, even with all this long-distance running I haven't yet been able to decide

what he means by this, although I'm just about beginning to
—and I don't like what it means. Because after all my thinking I found that it adds up to something that can't be true
about me, being born and brought up as I was. Because another thing people like the governor will never understand
is that I *am* honest, that I've never been anything else but
honest, and that I'll always be honest. Sounds funny. But it's
true because I know what honest means according to me and
he only knows what it means according to him: I think my
honesty is the only sort in the world, and he thinks his is the
only sort in the world as well. That's why this dirty great
walled-up and fenced-up manor house in the middle of nowhere
has been used to coop-up blokes like me. And if I had the
whip-hand I wouldn't even bother to build a place like this
to put all the cops, governors, posh whores, penpushers, army
officers, Members of Parliament in; no, I'd stick them up
against a wall and let them have it, like they'd have done
with blokes like us years ago, that is, if they'd ever known
what it means to be honest, which they don't and never will
so help me God Almighty.

I was nearly eighteen months in Borstal before I thought
about getting out. I can't tell you much about what it was like
there because I haven't got the hang of describing buildings
or saying how many crumby chairs and slatted windows make
a room. Neither can I do much complaining, because to tell
you the truth I didn't suffer in Borstal at all. I gave the same
answer a pal of mine gave when someone asked him how
much he hated it in the army. "I didn't hate it," he said.
"They fed me, gave me a suit, and pocket-money, which was
a bloody sight more than I ever got before, unless I worked
myself to death for it, and most of the time they wouldn't
let me work but sent me to the dole office twice a week." Well,

that's more or less what I say. Borstal didn't hurt me in that respect, so since I've got no complaints I don't have to describe what they gave us to eat, what the dorms were like, or how they treated us. But in another way Borstal does something to me. No, it doesn't get my back up, because it's always been up, right from when I was born. What it does do is show me what they've been trying to frighten me with. They've got other things as well, like prison and, in the end, the rope. It's like me rushing up to thump a man and snatch the coat off his back when, suddenly, I pull up because he whips out a knife and lifts it to stick me like a pig if I come too close. That knife is Borstal, clink, the rope. But once you've seen the knife you learn a bit of unarmed combat. You have to, because you'll never get that sort of knife in your own hands, and this unarmed combat doesn't amount to much. Still, there it is, and you keep on rushing up to this man, knife or not, hoping to get one of your hands on his wrist and the other on his elbow both at the same time, and press back until he drops the knife.

You see, by sending me to Borstal they've shown me the knife, and from now on I know something I didn't know before: that it's war between me and them. I always knew this, naturally, because I was in Remand Homes as well and the boys there told me a lot about their brothers in Borstal, but it was only touch and go then, like kittens, like boxing-gloves, like dobbie. But now that they've shown me the knife, whether I ever pinch another thing in my life again or not, I know who my enemies are and what war is. They can drop all the atom bombs they like for all I care: I'll never call it war and wear a soldier's uniform, because I'm in a different sort of war, that they think is child's play. The war they think is war is suicide, and those that go and get killed in war should be put in clink for attempted suicide because that's the feeling in blokes' minds when they rush to join up or let themselves be called up. I know, because I've thought how good it would be sometimes to do myself in and the easiest way to do it, it occurred to me, was to hope for a big war so's I could join up and get killed. But I got past that when I knew I already was in a war of my own, that I was born into one, that I grew up hearing the sound of 'old soldiers' who'd been over the top at Dartmoor, half-killed at Lincoln, trapped in no-man's-land at Borstal, that sounded louder than any Jerry bombs. Government wars aren't my wars; they've got nowt to do with me, because my own war's all that I'll ever be bothered about. I remember when I was fourteen and I went out into the country with three of my cousins, all about the same age, who later went to different Borstals, and then to different regiments, from which they soon deserted, and then to different gaols where they still are as far as I know. But anyway, we were all kids then, and wanted to go out to the woods for a change, to get away from the roads of stinking hot tar one summer. We climbed over fences and went through fields, scrumping a few sour apples on our way, until we saw the wood about a mile off. Up Colliers' Pad we heard another lot of kids talking in high-school voices behind a hedge. We crept up on them and peeped through the brambles, and saw they were eating a picnic, a real posh spread out of baskets and flasks and towels. There must have been about seven of them, lads and girls sent out by their mams and dads for the afternoon. So we went on our bellies through the hedge like crocodiles and surrounded them, and then dashed into the middle, scattering the fire and batting their tabs and snatching up all there was to eat, then running off over Cherry Orchard fields into the wood, with a man chasing us who'd come up while we were ransacking their picnic. We got away all right, and had a good feed into the bargain, because we'd been clambed to death and couldn't wait long enough to get our chops ripping into them thin lettuce and ham sandwiches and creamy cakes.

Well, I'll always feel during every bit of my life like those daft kids should have felt before we broke them up. But they never dreamed that what happened was going to happen, just like the governor of this Borstal who spouts. to us about honesty and all that wappy stuff don't know a bloody thing, while I know every minute of my life that a big boot is always likely to smash any nice picnic I might be barmy and dishonest enough to make for myself. I admit that there've been times when I've thought of telling the governor all this so as to put him on his guard, but when I've got as close as seeing him I've changed my mind, thinking to let him either find out for himself or go through the same mill as I've gone through. I'm not hard-hearted (in fact I've helped a few blokes in my time with the odd quid, lie, fag, or shelter from the rain when they've been on the run) but I'm boggered if I'm going to risk being put in the cells just for trying to give the governor a bit of advice he don't deserve. If my heart's soft I know the sort of people I'm going to save it for. And any advice I'd give the governor wouldn't do him the least bit of good; it'd only trip him up sooner than if he wasn't told at all, which I suppose is what I want to happen. But for the time being I'll let things go on as they are, which is something else I've learned in the last year or two. (It's a good job I can only think of these things as fast as I can write with this stub of pencil that's clutched in my paw, otherwise I'd have dropped the whole thing weeks ago.)

By the time I'm half-way through my morning course,

when after a frost-bitten dawn I can see a phlegmy bit of sun-light hanging from the bare twigs of beech and sycamore, and when I've measured my half-way mark by the short-cut scrim-mage down the steep bush-covered bank and into the sunken lane, when still there's not a soul in sight and not a sound except the neighing of a piebald foal in a cottage stable that I can't see, I get to thinking the deepest and daftest of all. The governor would have a fit if he could see me sliding down the bank because I could break my neck or ankle, but I can't not do it because it's the only risk I take and the only excitement I ever get, flying flat-out like one of them pterodactyls from the 'Lost World' I once heard on the wireless, crazy like a cut-balled cockerel, scratching myself to bits and almost letting myself go but not quite. It's the most wonderful minute because there's not one thought or word or picture of anything in my head while I'm going down. I'm empty, as empty as I was before I was born, and I don't let myself go, I suppose, because whatever it is that's farthest down inside me don't want me to die or hurt myself bad. And it's daft to think deep, you know, because it gets you nowhere, though deep is what I am when I've passed this half-way mark because the long-distance run of an early morning makes me think that every run like this is a life—a little life, I know—but a life as full of misery and happiness and things happening as you can ever get really around yourself—and I remember that after a lot of these runs I thought that it didn't need much know-how to tell how a life was going to end once it had got well started. But as usual I was wrong, caught first by the cops and then by my own bad brain, I could never trust myself to fly scot-free over these traps, was always tripped up sooner or later no matter how many I got over to the good without even knowing it. Looking back I suppose them big trees put their branches to their snouts and gave each other the wink, and there I was whizzing down the bank and not seeing a bloody thing.

II

I don't say to myself: "You shouldn't have done the job and then you'd have stayed away from Borstal"; no, what I ram into my runner-brain is that my luck had no right to scram just when I was on my way to making the coppers think I hadn't done the job after all. The time was autumn and the night foggy enough to set me and my mate Mike roaming the streets when we should have been rooted in front of the telly or stuck into a plush posh seat at the pictures, but I was restless after six weeks away from any sort of work, and well you might ask me why I'd been bone-idle for so long because normally I sweated my thin guts out on a milling-machine with the rest of them, but you see, my dad died from cancer of the throat, and mam collected a cool five hundred in insurance and benefits from the factory where he'd worked, "for your bereavement," they said, or words like that.

Now I believe, and my mam must have thought the same, that a wad of crisp blue-back fivers ain't a sight of good to a living soul unless they're flying out of your hand into some shopkeeper's till, and the shopkeeper is passing you tip-top things in exchange over the counter, so as soon as she got the money, mam took me and my five brothers and sisters out to town and got us dolled-up in new clothes. Then she ordered a twenty-one-inch telly, a new carpet because the old one was covered with blood from dad's dying and wouldn't wash out, and took a taxi home with bags of grub and a new fur coat.

And do you know—you wain't believe me when I tell you—
she'd still near three hundred left in her bulging handbag the
next day, so how could any of us go to work after that? Poor
old dad, he didn't get a look in, and he was the one who'd
done the suffering and dying for such a lot of lolly.

Night after night we sat in front of the telly with a ham
sandwich in one hand, a bar of chocolate in the other, and a
bottle of lemonade between our boots, while mam was with
some fancy-man upstairs on the new bed she'd ordered, and
I'd never known a family as happy as ours was in that couple
of months when we'd got all the money we needed. And
when the dough ran out I didn't think about anything much,
but just roamed the streets—looking for another job, I told
mam—hoping I suppose to get my hands on another five
hundred nicker so's the nice life we'd got used to could go on
and on for ever. Because it's surprising how quick you can
get used to a different life. To begin with, the adverts on the
telly had shown us how much more there was in the world to
buy than we'd ever dreamed of when we'd looked into shop
windows but hadn't seen all there was to see because we didn't
have the money to buy it with anyway. And the telly made
all these things seem twenty times better than we'd ever
thought they were. Even adverts at the cinema were cool and
tame, because now we were seeing them in private at home.
We used to cock our noses up at things in shops that didn't
move, but suddenly we saw their real value because they
jumped and glittered around the screen and had some pasty-
faced tart going head over heels to get her nail-polished
grabbers on to them or her lipstick lips over them, not like
the crumby adverts you saw on posters or in newspapers as
dead as doornails; these were flickering around loose, half-open
packets and tins, making you think that all you had to do was

finish opening them before they were yours, like seeing an unlocked safe through a shop window with the man gone away for a cup of tea without thinking to guard his lolly. The films they showed were good as well, in that way, because we couldn't get our eyes unglued from the cops chasing the robbers who had satchel-bags crammed with cash and looked like getting away to spend it—until the last moment. I always hoped they would end up free to blow the lot, and could never stop wanting to put my hand out, smash into the screen (it only looked a bit of rag-screen like at the pictures) and get the copper in a half-nelson so's he'd stop following the bloke with the money-bags. Even when he'd knocked off a couple of bank clerks I hoped he wouldn't get nabbed. In fact then I wished more than ever he wouldn't because it meant the hot-chair if he did, and I wouldn't wish that on anybody no matter what they'd done, because I'd read in a book where the hot-chair worn't a quick death at all, but that you just sat there scorching to death until you were dead. And it was when these cops were chasing the crooks that we played some good tricks with the telly, because when one of them opened his big gob to spout about getting their man I'd turn the sound down and see his mouth move like a goldfish or mackerel or a minnow mimicking what they were supposed to be acting—it was so funny the whole family nearly went into fits on the brand-new carpet that hadn't yet found its way to the bedroom. It was the best of all though when we did it to some Tory telling us about how good his government was going to be if we kept on voting for them—their slack chops rolling, opening and bumbling, hands lifting to twitch moustaches and touching their buttonholes to make sure the flower hadn't wilted, so that you could see they didn't mean a word they said, especially with not a murmur coming out because we'd cut off the sound. When the governor of the Borstal first talked to me I was reminded of those times so much that I nearly killed myself trying not to laugh. Yes, we played so many good stunts on the box of tricks that mam used to call us the Telly Boys, we got so clever at it.

My pal Mike got let off with probation because it was his first job—anyway the first they ever knew about—and because they said he would never have done it if it hadn't been for me talking him into it. They said I was a menace to honest lads like Mike—hands in his pockets so that they looked stone-empty, head bent forward as if looking for half-crowns to fill 'em with, a ripped jersey on and his hair falling into his eyes so that he could go up to women and ask them for a shilling because he was hungry—and that I was the brains behind the job, the guiding light when it came to making up anybody's mind, but I swear to God I worn't owt like that because really I ain't got no more brains than a gnat after hiding the money in the place I did. And I—being cranky like I am—got sent to Borstal because to tell you the honest truth I'd been to Remand Homes before—though that's another story and I suppose if ever I tell it it'll be just as boring as this one is. I was glad though that Mike got away with it, and I only hope he always will, not like silly bastard me.

So on this foggy night we tore ourselves away from the telly and slammed the front door behind us, setting off up our wide street like slow tugs on a river that'd broken their hooters, for we didn't know where the housefronts began what with the perishing cold mist all around. I was snatched to death without an overcoat: mam had forgotten to buy me one in the scrummage of shopping, and by the time I thought to remind her of it the dough was all gone. So we whistled 'The Teddy Boys Picnic' to keep us warm, and I told myself

that I'd get a coat soon if it was the last thing I did. Mike
said he thought the same about himself, adding that he'd also
get some brand-new glasses with gold rims, to wear instead
of the wire frames they'd given him at the school clinic years
ago. He didn't twig it was foggy at first and cleaned his
glasses every time I pulled him back from a lamp-post or car,
but when he saw the lights on Alfreton Road looking like
octopus eyes he put them in his pocket and didn't wear them
again until we did the job. We hadn't got two ha-pennies
between us, and though we weren't hungry we wished we'd
got a bob or two when we passed the fish and chip shops
because the delicious sniffs of salt and vinegar and frying fat
made our mouths water. I don't mind telling you we walked
the town from one end to the other and if our eyes worn't
glued to the ground looking for lost wallets and watches they
was swivelling around house windows and shop doors in case
we saw something easy and worth nipping into.

Neither of us said as much as this to each other, but I know
for a fact that that was what we was thinking. What I don't
know—and as sure as I sit here I know I'll never know—is
which of us was the first bastard to latch his peepers on to
that baker's backyard. Oh yes, it's all right me telling myself it
was me, but the truth is that I've never known whether it was
Mike or not, because I do know that I didn't see the open
window until he stabbed me in the ribs and pointed it out.
" See it? " he said.

" Yes," I told him, " so let's get cracking."

" But what about the wall though? " he whispered, looking
a bit closer.

" On your shoulders," I chipped in.

His eyes were already up there: " Will you be able to
reach? " It was the only time he ever showed any life.

"Leave it to me," I said, ever-ready. "I can reach anywhere from your ham-hock shoulders."

Mike was a nipper compared to me, but underneath the scruffy draught-board jersey he wore were muscles as hard as iron, and you wouldn't think to see him walking down the street with glasses on and hands in pockets that he'd harm a fly, but I never liked to get on the wrong side of him in a fight because he's the sort that don't say a word for weeks on end—sits plugged in front of the telly, or reads a cowboy book, or just sleeps—when suddenly BIFF—half kills somebody for almost nothing at all, such as beating him in a race for the last Football Post on a Saturday night, pushing in before him at a bus stop, or bumping into him when he was day-dreaming about Dolly-on-the-Tub next door. I saw him set on a bloke once for no more than fixing him in a funny way with his eyes, and it turned out that the bloke was cock-eyed but nobody knew it because he'd just that day come to live in our street. At other times none of these things would matter a bit, and I suppose the only reason why I was pals with him was because I didn't say much from one month's end to another either.

He puts his hands up in the air like he was being covered with a Gatling-Gun, and moved to the wall like he was going to be mowed down, and I climbed up him like he was a stile or step-ladder, and there he stood, the palms of his upshot maulers flat and turned out so's I could step on 'em like they was the adjustable jack-spanner under a car, not a sound of a breath nor the shiver of a flinch coming from him. I lost no time in any case, took my coat from between my teeth, chucked it up to the glass-topped wall (where the glass worn't too sharp because the jags had been worn down by years of accidental stones) and was sitting astraddle before I knew where I was. Then down the other side, with my legs rammed up into my throat when I hit the ground, the crack coming about as hard as when you fall after a high parachute drop, that one of my mates told me was like jumping off a twelve-foot wall, which this must have been. Then I picked up my bits and pieces and opened the gate for Mike, who was still grinning and full of life because the hardest part of the job was already done. "I came, I broke, I entered," like that clever-dick Borstal song.

I didn't think about anything at all, as usual, because I never do when I'm busy, when I'm draining pipes, looting sacks, yaling locks, lifting latches, forcing my bony hands and lanky legs into making something move, hardly feeling my lungs going in-whiff and out-whaff, not realizing whether my mouth is clamped tight or gaping, whether I'm hungry, itching from scabies, or whether my flies are open and flashing dirty words like muck and spit into the late-night final fog. And when I don't know anything about all this then how can I honest-to-God say I think of anything at such times? When I'm wondering what's the best way to get a window open or how to force a door, how can I be thinking or have anything on my mind? That's what the four-eyed white-smocked bloke with the note-book couldn't understand when he asked me questions for days and days after I got to Borstal; and I couldn't explain it to him then like I'm writing it down now; and even if I'd been able to maybe he still wouldn't have caught on because I don't know whether I can understand it myself even at this moment, though I'm doing my best you can bet.

So before I knew where I was I was inside the baker's office watching Mike picking up that cash box after he'd struck a match to see where it was, wearing a tailor-made fifty-shilling grin on his square crew-cut nut as his paws closed over the box like he'd squash it to nothing. "Out," he suddenly said, shaking it so's it rattled. "Let's scram."

"Maybe there's some more," I said, pulling half a dozen drawers out of a rollertop desk.

"No," he said, like he'd already been twenty years in the game, "this is the lot," patting his tin box, "this is it."

I pulled out another few drawers, full of bills, books and letters. "How do you know, you loony sod?"

He barged past me like a bull at a gate. "Because I do."

Right or wrong, we'd both got to stick together and do the same thing. I looked at an ever-loving babe of a brand-new typewriter, but knew it was too traceable, so blew it a kiss, and went out after him. "Hang on," I said, pulling the door to, "we're in no hurry."

"Not much we aren't," he says over his shoulder.

"We've got months to splash the lolly," I whispered as we crossed the yard, "only don't let that gate creak too much or you'll have the narks tuning-in."

"You think I'm barmy?" he said, creaking the gate so that the whole street heard.

I don't know about Mike, but now I started to think, of how we'd get back safe through the streets with that money-box up my jumper. Because he'd clapped it into my hand as soon as we'd got to the main road, which might have meant that he'd started thinking as well, which only goes to show how you don't know what's in anybody else's mind unless you think about things yourself. But as far as my thinking went at that moment it wasn't up to much, only a bit of fright that wouldn't budge not even with a hot blow-lamp, about what we'd say if a copper asked us where we were off to with that hump in my guts.

"What is it?" he'd ask, and I'd say: "A growth." "What do you mean, a growth, my lad?" he'd say back, narky like. I'd cough and clutch myself like I was in the most tripe-twisting pain in the world, and screw my eyes up like I was on my way to the hospital, and Mike would take my arm like he was the best pal I'd got. "Cancer," I'd manage to say to Narker, which would make his slow punch-drunk brain suspect a thing or two. "A lad of your age?" So I'd groan again, and hope to make him feel a real bully of a bastard, which would be impossible, but anyway: "It's in the family. Dad died of it last month, and I'll die of it next month by the feel of it." "What, did he have it in the guts?" "No, in the throat. But it's got me in the stomach." Groan and cough. "Well, you shouldn't be out like this if you've got cancer, you should be in the hospital." I'd get ratty now: "That's where I'm trying to go if only you'd let me and stop asking so many questions. Aren't I, Mike?" Grunt from Mike as he unslung his cosh. Then just in time the copper would tell us to get on our way, kind and considerate all of a sudden, saying that the outpatient department of the hospital closes at twelve, so hadn't he better call us a taxi? He would if we liked, he says, and he'd pay for it as well. But we tell him not to bother, that he's a good bloke even if he is a copper, that we know a short cut anyway. Then just as we're turning a corner he gets it into his big batchy head that we're going the opposite way to the hospital, and calls us back. So we'd start to run . . . if you can call all that thinking.

Up in my room Mike rips open that money-box with a hammer and chisel, and before we know where we are we've got seventy-eight pounds fifteen and fourpence ha'penny *each* lying all over my bed like tea spread out on Christmas Day: cake and trifle, salad and sandwiches, jam tarts and bars of chocolate: all shared and shared alike between Mike and me because we believed in equal work and equal pay, just like the comrades my dad was in until he couldn't do a stroke anymore and had no breath left to argue with. I thought how good it was that blokes like that poor baker didn't stash all his cash in one of the big marble-fronted banks that take up every corner of the town, how lucky for us that he didn't trust them no matter how many millions of tons of concrete or how many iron bars and boxes they were made of, or how many coppers kept their blue pop-eyed peepers glued on to them, how smashing it was that he believed in money-boxes when so many shopkeepers thought it old-fashioned and tried to be modern by using a bank, which wouldn't give a couple of sincere, honest, hardworking, conscientious blokes like Mike and me a chance.

Now you'd think, and I'd think, and anybody with a bit of imagination would think, that we'd done as clean a job as could ever be done, that, with the baker's shop being at least a mile from where we lived, and with not a soul having seen us, and what with the fog and the fact that we weren't more than five minutes in the place, that the coppers should never have been able to trace us. But then, you'd be wrong, I'd be wrong, and everybody else would be wrong, no matter how much imagination was diced out between us.

Even so, Mike and I didn't splash the money about, because that would have made people think straightaway that we'd latched on to something that didn't belong to us. Which wouldn't do at all, because even in a street like ours there are people who love to do a good turn for the coppers, though I never know why they do. Some people are so mean-gutted that even if they've only got tuppence more than you and they think you're the sort that would take it if you have half the chance, they'd get you put inside if they saw you ripping lead out of a lavatory, even if it weren't their lavatory—just to keep their tuppence out of your reach. And so we didn't do anything to let on about how rich we were, nothing like going down town and coming back dressed in brand-new Teddy boy suits and carrying a set of skiffle-drums like another pal of ours who'd done a factory office about six months before. No, we took the odd bobs and pennies out and folded the notes into bundles and stuffed them up the drainpipe outside the door in the backyard. "Nobody'll ever think of looking for it there," I said to Mike. "We'll keep it doggo for a week or two, then take a few quid a week out till it's all gone. We might be thieving bastards, but we're not green."

Some days later a plain-clothes dick knocked at the door. And asked for me. I was still in bed, at eleven o'clock, and had to unroll myself from the comfortable black sheets when I heard mam calling me. "A man to see you," she said. "Hurry up, or he'll be gone."

I could hear her keeping him at the back door, nattering about how fine it had been but how it looked like rain since early this morning—and he didn't answer her except to snap out a snotty yes or no. I scrambled into my trousers and wondered why he'd come—knowing it was a copper because ' a man to see you ' always meant just that in our house—and if I'd had any idea that one had gone to Mike's house as well at the same time I'd have twigged it to be because of that hundred and fifty quid's worth of paper stuffed up the drain-pipe outside the back door about ten inches away from that plain-clothed copper's boot, where mam still talked to him thinking she was doing me a favour, and I wishing to God she'd ask him in, though on second thoughts realizing that that would seem more suspicious than keeping him outside, because they know we hate their guts and smell a rat if they think we're trying to be nice to them. Mam wasn't born yesterday, I thought, thumping my way down the creaking stairs.

I'd seen him before: Borstal Bernard in nicky-hat, Remand Home Ronald in rowing-boat boots, Probation Pete in a pit-prop mackintosh, three-months clink in collar and tie (all this out of a Borstal skiffle-ballad that my new mate made up, and I'd tell you it in full but it doesn't belong in this story), a 'tec who'd never had as much in his pockets as that drainpipe had up its jackses. He was like Hitler in the face, right down to the paint-brush tash, except that being six-foot tall made him seem worse. But I straightened my shoulders to look into his illiterate blue eyes—like I always do with any copper.

Then he started asking me questions, and my mother from behind said: "He's never left that television set for the last three months, so you've got nowt on him, mate. You might as well look for somebody else, because you're wasting the rates you get out of my rent and the income-tax that comes out of my pay-packet standing there like that"—which was a laugh because she'd never paid either to my knowledge, and never would, I hoped.

"Well, you know where Papplewick Street is, don't you?" the copper asked me, taking no notice of mam.

"Ain't it off Alfreton Road?" I asked him back, helpful and bright.

"You know there's a baker's half-way down on the left-hand side, don't you?"

"Ain't it next door to a pub, then?" I wanted to know.

He answered me sharp: "No, it bloody well ain't." Coppers always lose their tempers as quick as this, and more often than not they gain nothing by it. "Then I don't know it," I told him, saved by the bell.

He slid his big boot round and round on the doorstep. "Where were you last Friday night?" Back in the ring, but this was worse than a boxing match.

I didn't like him trying to accuse me of something he wasn't sure I'd done. "Was I at that baker's you mentioned? Or in the pub next door?"

"You'll get five years in Borstal if you don't give me a straight answer," he said, unbuttoning his mac even though it was cold where he was standing.

"I was glued to the telly, like mam says," I swore blind. But he went on and on with his looney questions: "Have you got a television?"

The things he asked wouldn't have taken in a kid of two, and what else could I say to the last one except: "Has the aerial fell down? Or would you like to come in and see it?"

He was liking me even less for saying that. "We know you weren't listening to the television set last Friday, and so do you, don't you?"

"P'raps not, but I was *looking* at it, because sometimes we turn the sound down for a bit of fun." I could hear mam laughing from the kitchen, and I hoped Mike's mam was doing the same if the cops had gone to him as well.

"We know you weren't in the house," he said, starting up again, cranking himself with the handle. They always say 'We' 'We', never 'I' 'I'—as if they feel braver and righter knowing there's a lot of them against only one.

"I've got witnesses," I said to him. "Mam for one. Her fancy-man, for two. Ain't that enough? I can get you a dozen more, or thirteen altogether, if it was a baker's that got robbed."

"I don't want no lies," he said, not catching on about the baker's dozen. Where do they scrape cops up from anyway?

"All I want is to get from you where you put that money."

Don't get mad, I kept saying to myself, don't get mad—
hearing mam setting out cups and saucers and putting the
pan on the stove for bacon. I stood back and waved him inside
like I was a butler. "Come and search the house. If you've
got a warrant."

"Listen, my lad," he said, like the dirty bullying jumped-
up bastard he was, "I don't want too much of your lip, because
if we get you down to the Guildhall you'll get a few bruises
and black-eyes for your trouble." And I knew he wasn't kid-
ding either, because I'd heard about all them sort of tricks.
I hoped one day though that him and all his pals would be
the ones to get the black-eyes and kicks; you never knew. It
might come sooner than anybody thinks, like in Hungary.
"Tell me where the money is, and I'll get you off with
probation."

"What money?" I asked him, because I'd heard that one
before as well.

"You know what money."

"Do I look as though I'd know owt about money?" I said,
pushing my fist through a hole in my shirt.

"The money that was pinched, that you know all about,"
he said. "You can't trick me, so it's no use trying."

"Was it three-and-eightpence ha'penny?" I asked.

"You thieving young bastard. We'll teach you to steal
money that doesn't belong to you."

I turned my head around: "Mam," I called out, "get my
lawyer on the blower, will you?"

"Clever, aren't you?" he said in a very unfriendly way,
"but we won't rest until we clear all this up."

"Look," I pleaded, as if about to sob my socks off because
he'd got me wrong, "it's all very well us talking like this, it's

like a game almost, but I wish you'd tell me what it's all about, because honest-to-God I've just got out of bed and here you are at the door talking about me having pinched a lot of money, money that I don't know anything about."

He swung around now as if he'd trapped me, though I couldn't see why he might think so. "Who said anything about money? I didn't. What made you bring money into this little talk we're having?"

"It's you," I answered, thinking he was going barmy, and about to start foaming at the chops, "you've got money on the brain, like all policemen. Baker's shops as well."

He screwed his face up. "I want an answer from you: where's that money?"

But I was getting fed-up with all this. "I'll do a deal."

Judging by his flash-bulb face he thought he was suddenly on to a good thing. "What sort of a deal?"

So I told him: "I'll give you all the money I've got, one and fourpence ha'penny, if you stop this third-degree and let me go in and get my breakfast. Honest, I'm clambed to death. I ain't had a bite since yesterday. Can't you hear my guts rollin'?"

His jaw dropped, but on he went, pumping me for another half hour. A routine check-up, as they say on the pictures. But I knew I was winning on points.

Then he left, but came back in the afternoon to search the house. He didn't find a thing, not a French farthing. He asked me questions again and I didn't tell him anything except lies, lies, lies, because I can go on doing that forever without batting an eyelid. He'd got nothing on me and we both of us knew it, otherwise I'd have been down at the Guildhall in no time, but he kept on keeping on because I'd been in a Remand Home for a high-wall job before; and Mike was put through the same mill because all the local cops knew he was my best pal.

When it got dark me and Mike were in our parlour with a low light on and the telly off, Mike taking it easy in the rocking chair and me slouched out on the settee, both of us puffing a packet of Woods. With the door bolted and curtains drawn we talked about the dough we'd crammed up the drainpipe. Mike thought we should take it out and both of us do a bunk to Skegness or Cleethorpes for a good time in the arcades, living like lords in a boarding house near the pier, then at least we'd both have had a big beano before getting sent down.

"Listen, you daft bleeder," I said, "we aren't going to get caught at all, *and* we'll have a good time, later." We were so clever we didn't even go out to the pictures, though we wanted to.

In the morning old Hitler-face questioned me again, with one of his pals this time, and the next day they came, trying as hard as they could to get something out of me, but I didn't budge an inch. I know I'm showing off when I say this, but in me he'd met his match, and I'd never give in to questions no matter how long it was kept up. They searched the house a couple of times as well, which made me think they thought they really had something to go by, but I know now that they hadn't, and that it was all buckshee speculation. They turned the house upside down and inside out like an old sock, went from top to bottom and front to back but naturally didn't find a thing. The copper even poked his face up the front-room chimney (that hadn't been used or swept for years) and came down looking like Al Jolson so that he had to swill himself clean at the scullery sink. They kept tapping and pottering around the big aspidistra plant that grandma had left to mam, lifting it up from the table to look under the cloth, putting it aside so's they could move the table and get at the boards under the rug—but the big headed stupid ignorant bastards never once thought of emptying the soil out of the plant pot, where they'd have found the crumpled-up money-box that we'd buried the night we did the job. I suppose it's still there, now I think about it, and I suppose mam wonders now and again why the plant don't prosper like it used to—as if it could with a fistful of thick black tin lapped around its guts.

The last time he knocked at our door was one wet morning at five minutes to nine and I was sleep-logged in my crumby bed as usual. Mam had gone to work that day so I shouted for him to hold on a bit, and then went down to see who it was. There he stood, six-feet tall and sopping wet, and for the first time in my life I did a spiteful thing I'll never forgive myself for: I didn't ask him to come in out of the rain, because I wanted him to get double pneumonia and die. I suppose he could have pushed by me and come in if he'd wanted, but maybe he'd got used to asking questions on the doorstep and didn't want to be put off by changing his ground even though it was raining. Not that I don't like being spiteful because of any barmy principle I've got, but this bit of spite, as it turned out, did me no good at all. I should have treated him as a brother I hadn't seen for twenty years and dragged him in for a cup of tea and a fag, told him about the picture I hadn't seen the night before, asked him how his wife was after her operation and whether they'd shaved her moustache off to make it, and then sent him happy and satisfied out by the front door. But no, I thought, let's see what he's got to say for himself now.

He stood a little to the side of the door, either because it was less wet there, or because he wanted to see me from a different angle, perhaps having found it monotonous to watch a bloke's face always telling lies from the same side. "You've been identified," he said, twitching raindrops from his tash. "A woman saw you and your mate yesterday and she swears blind you are the same chaps she saw going into that bakery."

I was dead sure he was still bluffing, because Mike and I hadn't even seen each other the day before, but I looked worried. "She's a menace then to innocent people, whoever she is, because the only bakery I've been in lately is the one up our street to get some cut-bread on tick for mam."

He didn't bite on this. "So now I want to know where the money is"—as if I hadn't answered him at all.

"I think mam took it to work this morning to get herself some tea in the canteen." Rain was splashing down so hard I thought he'd get washed away if he didn't come inside. But I wasn't much bothered, and went on: "I remember I put it in the telly-vase last night—it was my only one-and-three and I was saving it for a packet of tips this morning—and I nearly had a jibbering black fit just now when I saw it had gone. I was reckoning on it for getting me through today because I don't think life's worth living without a fag, do you?"

I was getting into my stride and began to feel good, twigging that this would be my last pack of lies, and that if I kept it up for long enough this time I'd have the bastards beat: Mike and me would be off to the coast in a few weeks time having the fun of our lives, playing at penny football and latching on to a couple of tarts that would give us all they were good for. "And this weather's no good for picking-up fag-ends in the street," I said, "because they'd be sopping wet. Course, I know you could dry 'em out near the fire, but it don't taste the same you know, all said and done. Rainwater

does summat to 'em that don't bear thinkin' about: it turns
'em back into hoss-tods without the taste though."

I began to wonder, at the back of my brainless eyes, why
old copper-lugs didn't pull me up sharp and say he hadn't got
time to listen to all this, but he wasn't looking at me anymore,
and all my thoughts about Skegness went bursting to smither-
eens in my sludgy loaf. I could have dropped into the earth
when I saw what he'd fixed his eyes on.

He was looking at it, an ever-loving fiver, and I could only
jabber: "The one thing is to have some real fags because new
hoss-tods is always better than stuff that's been rained on
and dried, and I know how you feel about not being able to
find money because one-and-three's one-and-three in anybody's
pocket, and naturally if I see it knocking around I'll get you
on the blower tomorrow straightaway and tell you where you
can find it."

I thought I'd go down in a fit: three green-backs as well had
been washed down by the water, and more were following,
lying flat at first after their fall, then getting tilted at the
corners by wind and rainspots as if they were alive and wanted
to get back into the dry snug drainpipe out of the terrible
weather, and you can't imagine how I wished they'd be able
to. Old Hitler-face didn't know what to make of it but just
kept staring down and down, and I thought I'd better keep
on talking, though I knew it wasn't much good now.

"It's a fact, I know, that money's hard to come by and
half-crowns don't get found on bus seats or in dustbins, and
I didn't see any in bed last night because I'd 'ave known
about it, wouldn't I? You can't sleep with things like that in
the bed because they're too hard, and anyway at first they're.
. . . ." It took Hitler-boy a long time to catch on; they were
beginning to spread over the yard a bit, reinforced by the

third colour of a ten-bob note, before his hand clamped itself
on to my shoulder.

III

The pop-eyed potbellied governor said to a pop-eyed potbellied Member of Parliament who sat next to his pop-eyed
potbellied whore of a wife that I was his only hope for getting
the Borstal Blue Ribbon Prize Cup For Long Distance Cross
Country Running (All England), which I was, and it set me
laughing to myself inside, and I didn't say a word to any potbellied pop-eyed bastard that might give them real hope,
though I knew the governor anyway took my quietness to
mean he'd got that cup already stuck on the bookshelf in his
office among the few other mildewed trophies.

"He might take up running in a sort of professional way
when he gets out," and it wasn't until he'd said this and I'd
heard it with my own flap-tabs that I realized it might be
possible to do such a thing, run for money, trot for wages on
piece work at a bob a puff rising bit by bit to a guinea a gasp
and retiring through old age at thirty-two because of lace-
curtain lungs, a football heart, and legs like varicose bean-
stalks. But I'd have a wife and car and get my grinning long-
distance clock in the papers and have a smashing secretary to
answer piles of letters sent by tarts who'd mob me when they
saw who I was as I pushed my way into Woolworth's for a
packet of razor blades and a cup of tea. It was something to
think about all right, and sure enough the governor knew he'd
got me when he said, turning to me as if I would at any rate
have to be consulted about it all: "How does this matter strike
you, then, Smith, my lad?"

A line of potbellied pop-eyes gleamed at me and a row of

goldfish mouths opened and wiggled gold teeth at me, so I gave them the answer they wanted because I'd hold my trump card until later. "It'd suit me fine, sir," I said.

"Good lad. Good show. Right spirit. Splendid."

"Well," the governor said, "get that cup for us today and I'll do all I can for you. I'll get you trained so that you whack every man in the Free World." And I had a picture in my brain of me running and beating everybody in the world, leaving them all behind until only I was trot-trotting across a big wide moor alone, doing a marvellous speed as I ripped between boulders and reed-clumps, when suddenly: CRACK! CRACK! —bullets that can go faster than any man running, coming from a copper's rifle planted in a tree, winged me and split my gizzard in spite of my perfect running, and down I fell.

The potbellies expected me to say something else. "Thank you, sir," I said.

Told to go, I trotted down the pavilion steps, out on to the field because the big cross-country was about to begin and the two entries from Gunthorpe had fixed themselves early at the starting line and were ready to move off like white kangaroos. The sports ground looked a treat: with big tea-tents all round and flags flying and seats for families—empty because no mam or dad had known what opening day meant—and boys still running heats for the hundred yards, and lords and ladies walking from stall to stall, and the Borstal Boys Brass Band in blue uniforms; and up on the stands the brown jackets of Hucknall as well as our own grey blazers, and then the Gunthorpe lot with shirt sleeves rolled. The blue sky was full of sunshine and it couldn't have been a better day, and all of the big show was like something out of Ivanhoe that we'd seen on the pictures a few days before.

"Come on, Smith," Roach the sports master called to me,

"we don't want you to be late for the big race, eh? Although I dare say you'd catch them up if you were." The others cat-called and grunted at this, but I took no notice and placed myself between Gunthorpe and one of the Aylesham trusties, dropped on my knees and plucked a few grass blades to suck on the way round. So the big race it was, for them, watching from the grandstand under a fluttering Union Jack, a race for the governor, that he had been waiting for, and I hoped he and all the rest of his pop-eyed gang were busy placing big bets on me, hundred to one to win, all the money they had in their pockets, all the wages they were going to get for the next five years, and the more they placed the happier I'd be. Because here was a dead cert going to die on the big name they'd built for him, going to go down dying with laughter whether it choked him or not. My knees felt the cool soil pressing into them, and out of my eye's corner I saw Roach lift his hand. The Gunthorpe boy twitched before the signal was given; somebody cheered too soon; Medway bent forward; then the gun went, and I was away.

We went once around the field and then along a half-mile drive of elms, being cheered all the way, and I seemed to feel I was in the lead as we went out by the gate and into the lane, though I wasn't interested enough to find out. The five-mile course was marked by splashes of whitewash gleaming on gateposts and trunks and stiles and stones, and a boy with a waterbottle and bandage-box stood every half-mile waiting for those that dropped out or fainted. Over the first stile, without trying, I was still nearly in the lead but one; and if any of you want tips about running, never be in a hurry, and never let any of the other runners know you are in a hurry even if you are. You can always overtake on long-distance running with-out letting the others smell the hurry in you; and when you've

used your craft like this to reach the two or three up front
then you can do a big dash later that puts everybody else's
hurry in the shade because you've not had to make haste up
till then. I ran to a steady jog-trot rhythm, and soon it was so
smooth that I forgot I was running, and I was hardly able to
know that my legs were lifting and falling and my arms going
in and out, and my lungs didn't seem to be working at all, and
my heart stopped that wicked thumping I always get at the
beginning of a run. Because you see I never race at all; I just
run, and somehow I know that if I forget I'm racing and only
jog-trot along until I don't know I'm running I always win
the race. For when my eyes recognize that I'm getting near the
end of the course—by seeing a stile or cottage corner—I put
on a spurt, and such a fast big spurt it is because I feel that up
till then I haven't been running and that I've used up no
energy at all. And I've been able to do this because I've been
thinking; and I wonder if I'm the only one in the running
business with this system of forgetting that I'm running
because I'm too busy thinking; and I wonder if any of the
other lads are on to the same lark, though I know for a fact
that they aren't. Off like the wind along the cobbled footpath
and rutted lane, smoother than the flat grass track on the
field and better for thinking because it's not too smooth, and
I was in my element that afternoon knowing that nobody
could beat me at running but intending to beat myself before
the day was over. For when the governor talked to me of being
honest when I first came in he didn't know what the word
meant or he wouldn't have had me here in this race, trotting
along in shimmy and shorts and sunshine. He'd have had me
where I'd have had him if I'd been in his place: in a quarry
breaking rocks until he broke his back. At least old Hitler-
face the plain-clothes dick was honester than the governor,

because he at any rate had had it in for me and I for him, and when my case was coming up in court a copper knocked at our front door at four o'clock in the morning and got my mother out of bed when she was paralytic tired, reminding her she had to be in court at dead on half past nine. It was the finest bit of spite I've ever heard of, but I would call it honest, the same as my mam's words were honest when she really told that copper what she thought of him and called him all the dirty names she'd ever heard of, which took her half an hour and woke the terrace up.

I trotted on along the edge of a field bordered by the sunken lane, smelling green grass and honeysuckle, and I felt as though I came from a long line of whippets trained to run on two legs, only I couldn't see a toy rabbit in front and there wasn't a collier's cosh behind to make me keep up the pace. I passed the Gunthorpe runner whose shimmy was already black with sweat and I could just see the corner of the fenced-up copse in front where the only man I had to pass to win the race was going all out to gain the half-way mark. Then he turned into a tongue of trees and bushes where I couldn't see him anymore, and I couldn't see anybody, and I knew what the loneliness of the long-distance runner running across country felt like, realizing that as far as I was concerned this feeling was the only honesty and realness there was in the world and I knowing it would be no different ever, no matter what I felt at odd times, and no matter what anybody else tried to tell me. The runner behind me must have been a long way off because it was so quiet, and there was even less noise and movement than there had been at five o'clock of a frosty winter morning. It was hard to understand, and all I knew was that you had to run, run, run, without knowing why you were running, but on you went through fields you didn't understand and into woods that made you afraid, over hills without knowing you'd been up and down, and shooting across streams that would have cut the heart out of you had you fallen into them. And the winning post was no end to it, even though crowds might be cheering you in, because on you had to go before you got your breath back, and the only time you stopped really was when you tripped over a tree trunk and broke your neck or fell into a disused well and stayed dead in the darkness forever. So I thought: they aren't going to get me on this racing lark, this running and trying to win, this jog-trotting for a bit of blue ribbon, because it's not the way to go on at all, though they swear blind that it is. You should think about nobody and go your own way, not on a course marked out for you by people holding mugs of water and bottles of iodine in case you fall and cut yourself so that they can pick you up—even if you want to stay where you are—and get you moving again.

On I went, out of the wood, passing the man leading without knowing I was going to do so. Flip-flap, flip-flap, jog-trot, jog-trot, crunchslap-crunchslap, across the middle of a broad field again, rhythmically running in my greyhound effortless fashion, knowing I had won the race though it wasn't half over, won it if I wanted it, could go on for ten or fifteen or twenty miles if I had to and drop dead at the finish of it, which would be the same, in the end, as living an honest life like the governor wanted me to. It amounted to: win the race and be honest, and on trot-trotting I went, having the time of my life, loving my progress because it did me good and set me thinking which by now I liked to do, but not caring at all when I remembered that I had to win this race as well as run it. One of the two, I had to win the race or run it, and I knew I could do both because my legs had carried me well in front

—now coming to the short cut down the bramble bank and over the sunken road—and would carry me further because they seemed made of electric cable and easily alive to keep on slapping at those ruts and roots, but I'm not going to win because the only way I'd see I came in first would be if winning meant that I was going to escape the coppers after doing the biggest bank job of my life, but winning means the exact opposite, no matter how they try to kill or kid me, means running right into their white-gloved wall-barred hands and grinning mugs and staying there for the rest of my natural long life of stone-breaking anyway, but stone-breaking in the way I want to do it and not in the way they tell me.

Another honest thought that comes is that I could swing left at the next hedge of the field, and under its cover beat my slow retreat away from the sports ground winning post. I could do three or six or a dozen miles across the turf like this and cut a few main roads behind me so's they'd never know which one I'd taken; and maybe on the last one when it got dark I could thumb a lorry-lift and get a free ride north with somebody who might not give me away. But no, I said I wasn't daft didn't I? I won't pull out with only six months left, and besides there's nothing I want to dodge and run away from; I only want a bit of my own back on the In-laws and Potbellies by letting them sit up there on their big posh seats and watch me lose this race, though as sure as God made me I know that when I do lose I'll get the dirtiest crap and kitchen jobs in the months to go before my time is up. I won't be worth a threpp'ny-bit to anybody here, which will be all the thanks I get for being honest in the only way I know. For when the governor told me to be honest it was meant to be in his way not mine, and if I kept on being honest in the way he wanted and won my race for him he'd see I got the cushiest six months still left to run; but in my own way, well, it's not allowed, and if I find a way of doing it such as I've got now then I'll get what-for in every mean trick he can set his mind to. And if you look at it in my way, who can blame him? For this is war —and ain't I said so?—and when I hit him in the only place he knows he'll be sure to get his own back on me for not collaring that cup when his heart's been set for ages on seeing himself standing up at the end of the afternoon to clap me on the back as I take the cup from Lord Earwig or some such chinless wonder with a name like that. And so I'll hit him where it hurts a lot, and he'll do all he can to get his own back, tit for tat, though I'll enjoy it most because I'm hitting first, and because I planned it longer. I don't know why I think these thoughts are better than any I've ever had, but I do, and I don't care why. I suppose it took me a long time to get going on all this because I've had no time and peace in all my bandit life, and now my thoughts are coming pat and the only trouble is I often can't stop, even when my brain feels as if it's got cramp, frostbite and creeping paralysis all rolled into one and I have to give it a rest by slap-dashing down through the brambles of the sunken lane. And all this is another upper-cut I'm getting in first at people like the governor, to show how—if I can—his races are never won even though some bloke always comes unknowingly in first, how in the end the governor is going to be doomed while blokes like me will take the pickings of his roasted bones and dance like maniacs around his Borstal's ruins. And so this story's like the race and once again I won't bring off a winner to suit the governor; no, I'm being honest like he told me to, without him knowing what he means, though I don't suppose he'll ever come in with a story of his own, even if he reads this one of mine and knows who I'm talking about.

I've just come up out of the sunken lane, kneed and elbowed, thumped and bramble-scratched, and the race is two-thirds over, and a voice is going like a wireless in my mind saying that when you've had enough of feeling good like the first man on earth of a frosty morning, and you've known how it is to be taken bad like the last man on earth on a summer's afternoon, then you get at last to being like the only man on earth and don't give a bogger about either good or bad, but just trot on with your slippers slapping the good dry soil that at least would never do you a bad turn. Now the words are like coming from a crystal-set that's broken down, and something's happening inside the shell-case of my guts that bothers me and I don't know why or what to blame it on, a grinding near my ticker as though a bag of rusty screws is loose inside me and I shake them up every time I trot forward. Now and again I break my rhythm to feel my left shoulder-blade by swinging a right hand across my chest as if to rub the knife away that has somehow got stuck there. But I know it's nothing to bother about, that more likely it's caused by too much thinking that now and again I take for worry. For sometimes I'm the greatest worrier in the world I think (as you twigged I'll bet from me having got this story out) which is funny anyway because my mam don't know the meaning of the word so I don't take after her; though dad had a hard time of worry all his life up to when he filled his bedroom with hot blood and kicked the bucket that morning when nobody was in the house. I'll never forget it, straight I won't, because I was the one that found him and I often wished I hadn't. Back from a session on the fruit-machines at the fish-and-chip shop, jingling my three-lemon loot to a nail-dead house, as soon as I got in I knew something was wrong, stood leaning my head against the cold mirror above the mantelpiece trying not to open my eyes and see my stone-cold clock —because I knew I'd gone as white as a piece of chalk since coming in as if I'd been got at by a Dracula-vampire and even my penny-pocket winnings kept quiet on purpose.

Gunthorpe nearly caught me up. Birds were singing from the briar hedge, and a couple of thrushies flew like lightning into some thorny bushes. Corn had grown high in the next field and would be cut down soon with scythes and mowers; but I never wanted to notice much while running in case it put me off my stroke, so by the haystack I decided to leave it all behind and put on such a spurt, in spite of nails in my guts, that before long I'd left both Gunthorpe and the birds a good way off; I wasn't far now from going into that last mile and a half like a knife through margarine, but the quietness I suddenly trotted into between two pickets was like opening my eyes underwater and looking at the pebbles on a stream bottom, reminding me again of going back that morning to the house in which my old man had croaked, which is funny because I hadn't thought about it at all since it happened and even then I didn't brood much on it. I wonder why? I suppose that since I started to think on these long-distance runs I'm liable to have anything crop up and pester at my tripes and innards, and now that I see my bloody dad behind each grass-blade in my barmy runner-brain I'm not so sure I like to think and that it's such a good thing after all. I choke my phlegm and keep on running anyway and curse the Borstal-builders and their athletics—flappity-flap, slop-slop, crunch-slap-crunchslap-crunchslap—who've maybe got their own back on me from the bright beginning by sliding magic-lantern slides into my head that never stood a chance before. Only if I take whatever comes like this in my runner's stride can I keep on keeping on like my old self and beat them back; and now I've thought on this far I know I'll win, in the crunchslap end. So anyway after a bit I went upstairs one step at a time not thinking anything about how I should find dad and what I'd do when I did. But now I'm making up for it by going over the rotten life mam led him ever since I can remember, knocking-on with different men even when he was alive and fit and she not caring whether he knew it or not, and most of the time he wasn't so blind as she thought and cursed and roared and threatened to punch her tab, and I had to stand up to stop him even though I knew she deserved it. What a life for all of us. Well, I'm not grumbling, because if I did I might just as well win this bleeding race, which I'm not going to do, though if I don't lose speed I'll win it before I know where I am, and then where would I be?

Now I can hear the sportsground noise and music as I head back for the flags and the lead-in drive, the fresh new feel of underfoot gravel going against the iron muscles of my legs. I'm nowhere near puffed despite that bag of nails that rattles as much as ever, and I can still give a big last leap like gale-force wind if I want to, but everything is under control and I know now that there ain't another long-distance cross-country running runner in England to touch my speed and style. Our doddering bastard of a governor, our half-dead gangrened gaffer is hollow like an empty petrol drum, and he wants me and my running life to give him glory, to put in him blood and throbbing veins he never had, wants his potbellied pals to be his witnesses as I gasp and stagger up to his winning post so's he can say: "My Borstal gets that cup, you see. I win my bet, because it pays to be honest and try to gain the prizes I offer to my lads, and they know it, have known it all along. They'll always be honest now, because I made them so." And his pals will think: "He trains his lads to live right, after all;

he deserves a medal but we'll get him made a Sir "—and at this very moment as the birds come back to whistling I can tell myself I'll never care a sod what any of the chinless spineless In-laws think or say. They've seen me and they're cheering now and loudspeakers set around the field like elephant's ears are spreading out the big news that I'm well in the lead, and can't do anything else but stay there. But I'm still thinking of the Out-law death my dad died, telling the doctors to scat from the house when they wanted him to finish up in hospital (like a bleeding guinea-pig, he raved at them). He got up in bed to throw them out and even followed them down the stairs in his shirt though he was no more than skin and stick. They tried to tell him he'd want some drugs but he didn't fall for it, and only took the pain-killer that mam and I got from a herb-seller in the next street. It's not till now that I know what guts he had, and when I went into the room that morning he was lying on his stomach with the clothes thrown back, looking like a skinned rabbit, his grey head resting just on the edge of the bed, and on the floor must have been all the blood he'd had in his body, right from his toe-nails up, for nearly all of the lino and carpet was covered in it, thin and pink.

And down the drive I went, carrying a heart blocked up like Boulder Dam across my arteries, the nail-bag clamped down tighter and tighter as though in a woodwork vice, yet with my feet like birdwings and arms like talons ready to fly across the field except that I didn't want to give anybody that much of a show, or win the race by accident. I smell the hot dry day now as I run towards the end, passing a mountain-heap of grass emptied from cans hooked on to the fronts of lawn-mowers pushed by my pals; I rip a piece of tree-bark with my fingers and stuff it in my mouth, chewing wood and dust and maybe maggots as I run until I'm nearly sick, yet swallowing

what I can of it just the same because a little birdie whistled
to me that I've got to go on living for at least a bloody sight
longer yet but that for six months I'm not going to smell that
grass or taste that dusty bark or trot this lovely path. I hate to
have to say this but something bloody-well made me cry, and
crying is a thing I haven't bloody-well done since I was a kid
of two or three. Because I'm slowing down now for Gunthorpe
to catch me up, and I'm doing it in a place just where the
drive turns in to the sportsfield—where they can see what I'm
doing, especially the governor and his gang from the grandstand, and I'm going so slow I'm almost marking time. Those
on the nearest seats haven't caught on yet to what's happening and are still cheering like mad ready for when I make
that mark, and I keep on wondering when the bleeding hell
Gunthorpe behind me is going to nip by on to the field because
I can't hold this up all day, and I think Oh Christ it's just
my rotten luck that Gunthorpe's dropped out and that I'll be
here for half an hour before the next bloke comes up, but even
so, I say, I won't budge, I won't go for that last hundred yards
if I have to sit down cross-legged on the grass and have the
governor and his chinless wonders pick me up and carry me
there, which is against their rules so you can bet they'd never
do it because they're not clever enough to break the rules—
like I would be in their place—even though they are their own.
No, I'll show him what honesty means if it's the last thing I
do, though I'm sure he'll never understand because if he and
all them like him did it'd mean they'd be on my side which is
impossible. By God I'll stick this out like my dad stuck out his
pain and kicked them doctors down the stairs: if he had guts
for that then I've got guts for this and here I stay waiting for
Gunthorpe or Aylesham to bash that turf and go right slap-up
against that bit of clothes-line stretched across the winning

post. As for me, the only time I'll hit that clothes-line will be when I'm dead and a comfortable coffin's been got ready on the other side. Until then I'm a long-distance runner, crossing country all on my own no matter how bad it feels.

The Essex boys were shouting themselves blue in the face telling me to get a move on, waving their arms, standing up and making as if to run at that rope themselves because they were only a few yards to the side of it. You cranky lot, I thought, stuck at that winning post, and yet I knew they didn't mean what they were shouting, were really on my side and always would be, not able to keep their maulers to themselves, in and out of cop-shops and clink. And there they were now having the time of their lives letting themselves go in cheering me which made the governor think they were heart and soul on his side when he wouldn't have thought any such thing if he'd had a grain of sense. And I could hear the lords and ladies now from the grandstand, and could see them standing up to wave me in: " Run ! " they were shouting in their posh voices. " Run ! " But I was deaf, daft and blind, and stood where I was, still tasting the bark in my mouth and still blubbing like a baby, blubbing now out of gladness that I'd got them beat at last.

Because I heard a roar and saw the Gunthorpe gang throwing their coats up in the air and I felt the pat-pat of feet on the drive behind me getting closer and closer and suddenly a smell of sweat and a pair of lungs on their last gasp passed me by and went swinging on towards that rope, all shagged out and rocking from side to side, grunting like a Zulu that didn't know any better, like the ghost of me at ninety when I'm heading for that fat upholstered coffin. I could have cheered him myself: " Go on, go on, get cracking. Knot yourself up on that piece of tape." But he was already there, and so I went on, trot-trotting after him until I got to the rope, and collapsed, with a murderous sounding roar going up through my ears while I was still on the wrong side of it.

It's about time to stop; though don't think I'm not still running, because I am, one way or another. The governor at Borstal proved me right; he didn't respect my honesty at all; not that I expected him to, or tried to explain it to him, but if he's supposed to be educated then he should have more or less twigged it. He got his own back right enough, or thought he did, because he had me carting dustbins about every morning from the big full-working kitchen to the garden-bottoms where I had to empty them; and in the afternoon I spread out slops over spuds and carrots growing in the allotments. In the evenings I scrubbed floors, miles and miles of them. But it wasn't a bad life for six months, which was another thing he could never understand and would have made it grimmer if he could, and it was worth it when I look back on it, considering all the thinking I did, and the fact that the boys caught on to me losing the race on purpose and never had enough good words to say about me, or curses to throw out (to themselves) at the governor.

The work didn't break me; if anything it made me stronger in many ways, and the governor knew, when I left, that his spite had got him nowhere. For since leaving Borstal they tried to get me in the army, but I didn't pass the medical and I'll tell you why. No sooner was I out, after that final run and six-months hard, that I went down with pleurisy, which means as far as I'm concerned that I lost the governor's race all right, and won my own twice over, because I know for certain that if I hadn't raced my race I wouldn't have got this pleurisy, which keeps me out of khaki but doesn't stop me doing the sort of work my itchy fingers want to do.

I'm out now and the heat's switched on again, but the rats haven't got me for the last big thing I pulled. I counted six hundred and twenty-eight pounds and am still living off it because I did the job all on my own, and after it I had the peace to write all this, and it'll be money enough to keep me going until I finish my plans for doing an even bigger snatch, something up my sleeve I wouldn't tell to a living soul. I worked out my systems and hiding-places while pushing scrubbing-brushes around them Borstal floors, planned my out-ward life of innocence and honest work, yet at the same time grew perfect in the razor-edges of my craft for what I knew I had to do once free; and what I'll do again if netted by the poaching coppers.

In the meantime (as they say in one or two books I've read since, useless though because all of them ended on a winning post and didn't teach me a thing) I'm going to give this story to a pal of mine and tell him that if I do get captured again by the coppers he can try and get it put into a book or something, because I'd like to see the governor's face when he reads it, if he does, which I don't suppose he will; even if he did read it though I don't think he'd know what it was all about. And if I don't get caught the bloke I give this story to will never give me away; he's lived in our terrace for as long as I can remember, and he's my pal. That I do know.

Uncle Ernest

A MIDDLE-AGED man wearing a dirty raincoat, who badly needed a shave and looked as though he hadn't washed for a month, came out of a public lavatory with a cloth bag of tools folded beneath his arm. Standing for a moment on the edge of the pavement to adjust his cap—the cleanest thing about him—he looked casually to left and right and, when the flow of traffic had eased off, crossed the road. His name and trade were always spoken in one breath, even when the nature of his trade was not in question: Ernest Brown the upholsterer. Every night before returning to his lodgings he left the bag of tools for safety with a man who looked after the public lavatory near the town centre, for he felt there was a risk of them being lost or stolen should he take them back to his room, and if such a thing were to happen his living would be gone.

Chimes to the value of half past ten boomed from the Council-house clock. Over the theatre patches of blue sky held hard-won positions against autumnal clouds, and a treacherous wind lashed out its gusts, sending paper and cigarette packets cartwheeling along unswept gutters. Empty-bellied Ernest was ready for his breakfast, so walked through a café doorway, instinctively lowering his head as he did so, though the beams were a foot above his height.

The long spacious eating-place was almost full. Ernest usually arrived for his breakfast at nine o'clock, but having been paid ten pounds for re-covering a three-piece in a public house the day before, he had stationed himself in the Saloon Bar for the rest of the evening to drink jar after jar of beer, in a slow prolonged and concentrated way that lonely men have. As a result it had been difficult to drag himself from drugged and blissful sleep this morning. His face was pale and his eyes an unhealthy yellow: when he spoke only a few solitary teeth showed behind his lips.

Having passed through the half dozen noisy people standing about he found himself at the counter, a scarred and chipped haven for hands, like a littered invasion beach extending between two headlands of tea-urns. The big fleshy brunette was busy, so he hastily scanned the list written out in large white letters on the wall behind. He made a timid gesture with his hand. "A cup of tea, please."

The brunette turned on him. Tea swilled from a huge brown spout—into a cup that had a crack emerging like a hair above the layer of milk—and a spoon clinked after it into the steam. "Anything else?"

He spoke up hesitantly. "Tomatoes on toast as well." Picking up the plate pushed over to him he moved slowly backwards out of the crowd, then turned and walked towards a vacant corner table.

A steamy appetizing smell rose from the plate: he took up the knife and fork and, with the sharp clean action of a craftsman, cut off a corner of the toast and tomato and raised it slowly to his mouth, eating with relish and hardly noticing people sitting roundabout. Each wielding of his knife and fork, each geometrical cut of the slice of toast, each curve and twist of his lips joined in a complex and regular motion that gave him great satisfaction. He ate slowly, quietly and contentedly, aware only of himself and his body being warmed and made tolerable once more by food. The leisurely movement of spoon and cup and saucer made up the familiar noise of late breakfast in a crowded café, sounded like music flowing here and there in variations of rhythm.

For years he had eaten alone, but was not yet accustomed to loneliness. He could not get used to it, had only adapted himself to it temporarily in the hope that one day its spell would break. Ernest remembered little of his past, and life moved under him so that he hardly noticed its progress. There was no strong memory to entice him to what had gone by, except that of dead and dying men straggling barbed-wire between the trenches in the first world war. Two sentences had dominated his lips during the years that followed: "I should not be here in England. I should be dead with the rest of them in France." Time bereft him of these sentences, till only a dull wordless image remained.

People, he found, treated him as if he were a ghost, as if he were not made of flesh and blood—or so it seemed—and from then on he had lived alone. His wife left him—due to his too vile temper, it was said—and his brothers went to other towns. Later he had thought to look them up, but decided against it: for even in this isolation only the will to go forward and accept more of it seemed worth while. He felt in a dim indefinite way that to go back and search out the slums and landmarks of his youth, old friends, the smells and sounds that beckoned him tangibly from better days, was a sort of death. He argued that it was best to leave them alone, because it seemed somehow probable that after death —whenever it came—he would meet all these things once again.

No pink scar marked his flesh from shell-shock and a jolted brain, and so what had happened in the war warranted no

pension book, and even to him the word 'injury' never came
into his mind. It was just that he did not care anymore: the
wheel of the years had broken him, and so had made life
tolerable. When the next war came his back was not burdened
at first, and even the fines and days in prison that he was made
to pay for being without Identity Card or Ration Book—or
for giving them away with a glad heart to deserters—did not
lift him from his tolerable brokenness. The nightmare hours
of gunfire and exploding bombs revived a dull image long
suppressed as he stared blankly at the cellar wall of his boarding house, and even threw into his mind the scattered words
of two insane sentences. But, considering the time-scale his
life was lived on, the war ended quickly, and again nothing
mattered. He lived from hand to mouth, working cleverly at
settees and sofas and chairs, caring about no one. When work
was difficult to find and life was hard, he did not notice it very
much, and now that he was prosperous and had enough
money, he also detected little difference, spending what he
earned on beer, and never once thinking that he needed a new
coat or a solid pair of boots.

He lifted the last piece of toast and tomato from his plate,
then felt dregs of tea moving against his teeth. When he had
finished chewing he lit a cigarette and was once more aware
of people sitting around him. It was eleven o'clock and the
low-roofed café was slowly emptying, leaving only a dozen
people inside. He knew that at one table they were talking
about horse-racing and at another about war, but words only
flowed into his ears and entered his mind at a low pitch of
comprehension, leaving it calm and content as he vaguely
contemplated the positions and patterns of tables about the
room. There would be no work until two o'clock, so he
intended sitting where he was until then. Yet a sudden em-

barrassment at having no food on the table to justify a prolonged occupation of it sent him to the counter for tea and cakes.

As he was being served two small girls came in. One sat at a table, but the second and elder stood at the counter. When he returned to his place he found the younger girl sitting there. He was confused and shy, but nevertheless sat down to drink tea and cut a cake into four pieces. The girl looked at him and continued to do so until the elder one came from the counter carrying two cups of steaming tea.

They sat talking and drinking, utterly oblivious of Ernest, who slowly felt their secretive, childish animation enter into himself. He glanced at them from time to time, feeling as if he should not be there, though when he looked at them he did so in a gentle way, with kind, full-smiling eyes. The elder girl, about twelve years old, was dressed in a brown coat that was too big for her, and though she was talking and laughing most of the time he noticed the paleness of her face and her large round eyes that he would have thought beautiful had he not detected the familiar type of vivacity that expressed neglect and want.

The smaller girl was less lively and merely smiled as she answered her sister with brief curt words. She drank her tea and warmed her hands at the same time without putting the cup down once until she had emptied it. Her thin red fingers curled around the cup as she stared into the leaves, and gradually the talk between them died down and they were silent, leaving the field free for traffic that could be heard moving along the street outside, and for inside noises made by the brunette who washed cups and dishes ready for the rush that was expected at midday dinner-time.

Ernest was calculating how many yards of rexine would be

needed to cover the job he was to do that afternoon, but when
the younger girl began speaking he listened to her, hardly
aware that he was doing so.

"If you've got any money I'd like a cake, our Alma."

"I haven't got any more money," the elder one replied
impatiently.

"Yes you have, and I'd like a cake."

She was adamant, almost aggressive. "Then you'll have to
want on, because I've only got tuppence."

"You can buy a cake with that," the young girl persisted,
twining her fingers around the empty cup. "We don't need
bus fares home because it ain't far to walk."

"We can't walk home: it might rain."

"No it won't."

"Well I want a cake as well, but I'm not walking all that
way," the elder girl said conclusively, blocking any last gap
that might remain in her defences. The younger girl gave up
and said nothing, looked emptily in front of her.

Ernest had finished eating and took out a cigarette, struck
a match across the iron fastening of a table leg and, having
inhaled deeply, allowed smoke to wander from his mouth.
Like a gentle tide washing in under the moon, a line of water
flowing inwards and covering the sand, a feeling of acute
loneliness took hold of him, an agony that would not let him
weep. The two girls sat before him wholly engrossed in themselves, still debating whether they should buy a cake, or
whether they should ride home on a bus.

"But it'll be cold," reasoned the elder, "walking home."

"No it won't," the other said, but with no conviction in
her words. The sound of their voices told him how lonely he
was, each word feeding him with so much more loneliness that
he felt utterly unhappy and empty.

Time went slowly: the minute-hand of the clock seemed as if it were nailed immovably at one angle. The two girls looked at each other and did not notice him: he withdrew into himself and felt the emptiness of the world and wondered how he would spend all the days that seemed to stretch vacantly, like goods on a broken-down conveyor belt, before him. He tried to remember things that had happened and felt panic when he discovered a thirty-year vacuum. All he could see behind was a grey mist and all he could see before him was the same unpredictable fog that would hide nothing. He wanted to walk out of the café and find some activity so that he would henceforth be able to mark off the passage of his empty days, but he had no will to move. He heard someone crying so shook himself free of such thoughts and saw the younger girl with hands to her eyes, weeping. "What's the matter?" he asked tenderly, leaning across the table.

The elder girl replied for her, saying sternly:

"Nothing. She's acting daft."

"But she must be crying for some reason. What is it?" Ernest persisted, quietly and soothingly, bending closer still towards her. "Tell me what's wrong." Then he remembered something. He drew it like a live thread from a mixture of reality and dream, hanging on to vague words that floated back into his mind. The girls' conversation came to him through an intricate process of recollection. "I'll get you something to eat," he ventured. "Can I?"

She unscrewed clenched fingers from her eyes and looked up, while the elder girl glared at him resentfully and said: "We don't want anything. We're going now."

"No, don't go," he cried. "You just sit down and see what I'm going to get for you." He stood up and walked to the counter, leaving them whispering to each other.

He came back with a plate of pastries and two cups of tea, which he set before the girls, who looked on in silence. The younger was smiling now. Her round eager eyes were fascinated, yet followed each movement of his hands with some apprehension. Though still hostile the elder girl was gradually subdued by the confidently working actions of his hands, by caressing words and the kindness that showed in his face. He was wholly absorbed in doing good and, at the same time, fighting the feeling of loneliness that he still remembered, but only as a nightmare is remembered.

The two children fell under his spell, began to eat cakes and sip the tea. They glanced at each other, and then at Ernest as he sat before them smoking a cigarette. The café was still almost empty, and the few people eating were so absorbed in themselves, or were in so much of a hurry to eat their food and get out that they took little notice of the small company in the corner. Now that the atmosphere between himself and the two girls had grown more friendly Ernest began to talk to them. "Do you go to school?" he asked.

The elder girl automatically assumed control and answered his questions. "Yes, but today we had to come down town on an errand for our mam."

"Does your mother go out to work, then?"

"Yes," she informed him. "All day."

Ernest was encouraged. "And does she cook your dinners?"

She obliged him with another answer. "Not until night."

"What about your father?" he went on.

"He's dead," said the smaller girl, her mouth filled with food, daring to speak outright for the first time. Her sister looked at her with disapproval, making it plain that she had said the wrong thing and that she should only speak under guidance.

"Are you going to school then this afternoon?" Ernest resumed.

"Yes," the spokesman said.

He smiled at her continued hard control. "And what's your name then?"

"Alma," she told him, "and hers is Joan." She indicated the smaller girl with a slight nod of the head.

"Are you often hungry?"

She stopped eating and glanced at him, uncertain how to answer. "No, not much," she told him non-committally, busily eating a second pastry.

"But you were today?"

"Yes," she said, casting away diplomacy like the crumpled cake-paper she let fall to the floor.

He said nothing for a few moments, sitting with knuckles pressed to his lips. "Well, look"—he began suddenly talking again—"I come in here every day for my dinner, just about half past twelve, and if ever you're feeling hungry, come down and see me."

They agreed to this, accepted sixpence for their bus fares home, thanked him very much, and said good-bye.

During the following weeks they came to see him almost every day. Sometimes, when he had little money, he filled his empty stomach with a cup of tea while Alma and Joan satisfied themselves on five shillings'-worth of more solid food. But he was happy and gained immense satisfaction from seeing them bending hungrily over eggs, bacon and pastries, and he was so smoothed at last into a fine feeling of having something to live for that he hardly remembered the lonely days when his only hope of being able to talk to someone was by going into a public house to get drunk. He was happy now because he had his 'little girls' to look after, as he came to call them.

He began spending all his money to buy them presents, so that he was often in debt at his lodgings. He still did not buy any clothes, for whereas in the past his money had been swilled away on beer, now it was spent on presents and food for the girls, and he went on wearing the same old dirty mackintosh and was still without a collar to his shirt; even his cap was no longer clean.

Every day, straight out of school, Alma and Joan ran to catch a bus for the town centre and, a few minutes later, smiling and out of breath, walked into the café where Ernest was waiting. As days and weeks passed, and as Alma noticed how much Ernest depended on them for company, how happy he was to see them, and how obviously miserable when they did not come for a day—which was rare now—she began to demand more and more presents, more food, more money, but only in a particularly naïve and childish way, so that Ernest, in his oblivious contentment, did not notice it.

But certain customers of the café who came in every day could not help but see how the girls asked him to buy them this and that, and how he always gave in with a nature too good to be decently true, and without the least sign of realizing what was really happening. He would never dream to question their demands, for to him, these two girls whom he looked upon almost as his own daughters were the only people he had to love.

Ernest, about to begin eating, noticed two smartly dressed men sitting at a table a few yards away. They had sat in the same place the previous day, and also the day before that, but he thought no more about it because Joan and Alma came in and walked quickly across to his table.

"Hello, Uncle Ernest!" they said brightly. "What can we have for dinner?" Alma looked across at the chalk-written list on the wall to read what dishes were available.

His face changed from the blank preoccupation of eating, and a smile of happiness infused his cheeks, eyes, and the curve of his lips. "Whatever you like," he answered.

"But what have they got?" Alma demanded crossly. "I can't read their scrawl."

"Go up to the counter and ask for a dinner," he advised with a laugh.

"Will you give me some money then?" she asked, her hand out. Joan stood by without speaking, lacking Alma's confidence, her face timid, and nervous because she did not yet understand this regular transaction of money between Ernest and themselves, being afraid that one day they would stand there waiting for money and Ernest would quite naturally look surprised and say there was nothing for them.

He had just finished repairing an antique three-piece and had been paid that morning, so Alma took five shillings and they went to the counter for a meal. While they were waiting to be served the two well-dressed men who had been watching Ernest for the last few days stood up and walked over to him.

Only one of them spoke; the other held his silence and looked on. "Are those two girls your daughters, or any relation to you?" the first asked, nodding towards the counter.

Ernest looked up and smiled. "No," he explained in a mild voice, "they're just friends of mine, why?"

The man's eyes were hard, and he spoke clearly. "What kind of friends?"

"Just friends. Why? Who are you?" He shuddered, feeling a kind of half-guilt growing inside him for a half-imagined reason that he hoped wasn't true.

"Never mind who we are. I just want you to answer my question."

Ernest raised his voice slightly, yet did not dare to look into the man's arrogant eyes. "Why? " he cried. "What's it got to do with you? Why are you asking questions like this? "

"We're from the police station," the man remarked dryly, "and we've had complaints that you're giving these little girls money and leading them the wrong way! "

Ernest wanted to laugh, but only from misery. Yet he did not want to laugh in case he should annoy the two detectives. He started to talk: "But . . . but . . ."—then found himself unable to go on. There was much that he wanted to say, yet he could enunciate nothing, and a bewildered animal stare moved slowly into his eyes.

"Look," the man said emphatically, "we don't want any of your 'buts'. We know all about you. We know who you are. We've known you for years in fact, and we're asking you to leave those girls alone and have nothing more to do with them. Men like you shouldn't give money to little girls. You should know what you're doing, and have more sense."

Ernest protested loudly at last. "I tell you they're friends of mine. I mean no harm. I look after them and give them presents just as I would daughters of my own. They're the only company I've got. In any case why shouldn't I look after them? Why should you take them away from me? Who do you think you are? Leave me alone . . . leave me alone." His voice had risen to a weak scream of defiance, and the other people in the crowded café were looking around and staring at him, wondering what was the cause of the disturbance.

The two detectives acted quickly and competently, yet without apparent haste. One stood on each side of him, lifted him up, and walked him by the counter, out on to the street, squeezing his wrists tightly as they did so. As Ernest passed the counter he saw the girls holding their plates, looking in fear and wonder at him being walked out.

They took him to the end of the street, and stood there for a few seconds talking to him, still keeping hold of his wrists and pressing their fingers hard into them.

"Now look here, we don't want any more trouble from you, but if ever we see you near those girls again, you'll find yourself up before a magistrate." The tone of finality in his voice possessed a physical force that pushed Ernest to the brink of sanity.

He stood speechless. He wanted to say so many things, but the words would not come to his lips. They quivered helplessly with shame and hatred, and so were incapable of making words. "We're asking you in a peaceful manner," the detective went on, "to leave them alone. Understand?"

"Yes," Ernest was forced to answer.

"Right. Go on then. And we don't want to see you with those girls again."

He was only aware of the earth sliding away from under his feet, and a wave of panic crashing into his mind, and he felt the unbearable and familiar emptiness that flowed outwards from a tiny and unknowable point inside him. Then he was filled with hatred for everything, then intense pity for all the movement that was going on around him, and finally even more intense pity for himself. He wanted to cry but could not: he could only walk away from his shame.

Then he began to shed agony at each step. His bitterness eddied away and a feeling the depth of which he had never known before took its place. There was now more purpose in the motion of his footsteps as he went along the pavement through midday crowds. And it seemed to him that he did not care about anything any more as he pushed through the swing doors and walked into the crowded and noisy bar of a public house, his stare fixed by a beautiful heavily baited trap of beer pots that would take him into the one and only best kind of oblivion.

Mr. Raynor the School-teacher

NOW that the boys were relatively quiet Mr. Raynor looked out of the classroom window, across the cobbled road and into the window of Harrison's the draper's shop. With sight made keener by horn-rimmed spectacles he observed the new girl lift her arms above her head to reach some small drawers of cotton, an action which elongated the breasts inside her dark blue dress until she looked almost flat-chested. Mr. Raynor rasped his shoes slightly on the bar of his tall stool, a stool once the subject of a common-room joke, which said that he had paid the caretaker well to put on longer legs so that he could see better out of the window and observe with more ease the girls in Harrison's shop across the road. Most of the boys before him had grown so used to his long periods of distraction—freedom for them—that they no longer found inclination or time to sneer at the well-known reason for it.

When the flat-chested girl went upstairs into the Men's Suits, another girl, small, heavy, and with a satisfyingly larger bosom, came into the centre span of the counter and spread out a box of coloured ties like wheel-spokes before a man who had just come in. But her appeal to his taste was still at an unpalatable extreme, and he again regretted the departure of a girl who had been, to him, perfect in every way. Against a background of road and shop, and movements between the two that his fixed stare kept easily in a state of insignificance, he recalled her image, a difficult thing because faces did not linger clearly for a long time in his memory, even though she had been dead only ten days.

Eighteen, he remembered her, and not too tall, with almost masculine features below short chestnut hair: brown eyes, full cheeks and proportionate lips, like Aphrodite his inward eye had commented time and time again, only a little sweeter. She wore brown sweater and brown cardigan, a union that gave only tormenting glimpses of her upper figure, until one summer's day when the cardigan was set aside, revealing breasts on the same classical style, hips a trifle broad, complementing nevertheless her somewhat stocky legs and fleshy redeeming calves. She had only to move from the counter to the foot of the stairs that led to the upper part of the shop, and Mr. Raynor's maxims of common arithmetic became stale phrases of instruction to be given out quickly, leaving his delighted class with an almost free session.

What memory could not accomplish, imagination did, and he recreated a tangible image, moved by long-cultivated preoccupations of sensuality in which his wife and family took no part. He adjusted his spectacles, rolled his tongue around the dry back of his teeth, and grated his feet once more on the bar of the chair. As she walked she had carried her whole body in a sublime movement conducive to the attraction of every part of it, so that he was even aware of heels inside her shoes and finger-tips buried perhaps beneath a bolt of opulent cloth. A big trolley-bus bundled its green-fronted track along the road, and carried his vision away on the coloured advertisements decorating the band between top and bottom deck.

Deprived so suddenly he felt for a cigarette, but there was half an hour yet for the playtime break. And he still had to deal with the present class before they went to geography at ten o'clock. The noise broke into him, sunk him down to reality like cold water entering a ship. They were the eldest rag-mob of the school, and the most illiterate, a C stream of fourteen-year-old louts rearing to leave and start work at the factories round about. Bullivant the rowdiest subsided only after his head was well turned from the window; but the noise went on. The one feasible plan was to keep them as quiet as possible for the remaining months, then open the gates and let them free, allow them to spill out into the big wide world like the young animals they were, eager for fags and football, beer and women and a forest of streets to roam in. The responsibility would be no longer his, once they were packed away with the turned pages of his register into another, more incorrigible annexe than the enclave of jungle he ruled for his living. He would have done whatever could be done with such basically unsuitable and unwilling scholars.

" All right," he called out in a loud clear voice, " let's have a little quietness in the room." Though the noise persisted, an air of obedience reigned. Mr. Raynor was not a strict disciplinarian, but he had taught for twenty-five years, and so acquired a voice of authority that was listened to. Even if he didn't hit them very often, it was realized that he was not a young man and could easily do so. And it was consciously felt that there was more force behind a middle-aged fist than a young and inexperienced one. Consequently when he told them to keep quiet, they usually did.

"Take out your Bibles," he said, "and open them at Exodus, chapter six."

He watched forty-five hands, few of them clean, unaccountably opening the Bible, as they did all books, from the back and working to the front. Now and again he caught the flicker of brightly coloured illustrations at different points in the class, on their way through a welter of pages. He leaned forward on the high desk, one elbow supporting his forehead, seeing Bullivant whisper to the boy next to him, and hearing the boy giggle.

"Handley," Mr. Raynor demanded with a show of sternness, "who was Aaron?"

A small boy from the middle of the class stood up: "Aaron from the Bible, sir?"

"Yes. Who else, you ass?"

"Don't know, sir," the boy answered, either because he really didn't, Mr. Raynor told himself, or by way of revenge for being called an ass.

"Didn't you read the chapter yesterday I told you to read?"

Here was a question he could answer. "Yes, sir," came the bright response.

"Well then, who was Aaron?"

His face was no longer bright. It became clouded as he admitted: "I've forgot, sir."

Mr. Raynor ran a hand slowly over his forehead. He changed tack. "NO!" he yelled, so loudly that the boy jumped. "Don't sit down yet, Handley." He stood up again. "We've been reading this part of the Bible for a month, so you should be able to answer my question. Now: Who was the brother of Moses?"

Bullivant chanted from behind:

> "Then the Lord said unto Moses
> All the Jews shall have long noses
> Exceptin' Aaron
> He shall 'ave a square 'un
> And poor old Peter
> He shall 'ave a gas-meter!"

The low rumble reached Mr. Raynor, and he saw several half-tortured faces around Bullivant trying not to laugh. "Tell me, Handley," he said again, "who was the brother of Moses?"

Handley's face became happy, almost recognizable under the unfamiliar light of inspiration, for the significance of the chanted verse had eaten its way through to his understanding. "Aaron, sir," he said.

"And so"—Mr. Raynor assumed he was getting somewhere at last—"who was Aaron?"

Handley, who had considered his ordeal to be over on hearing a subdued cheer of irony from Bullivant, lifted a face blank in defeat. "Don't know, sir."

A sigh of frustration, not allowed to reach the boys, escaped Mr. Raynor. "Sit down," he said to Handley, who did so with such alacrity that the desk lid rattled. Duty had been done as far as Handley was concerned, and now it was Robinson's turn, who stood up from his desk a few feet away. "Tell us who Aaron was," Mr. Raynor ordered.

Robinson was a brighter boy, who had thought to keep a second Bible open beneath his desk lid for reference. "A priest, sir," he answered sharply, "the brother of Moses."

"Sit down, then," Mr. Raynor said. "Now, remember that, Handley. What House are you in, Robinson?"

He stood up again, grinning respectfully. "Buckingham, sir."

"Then take a credit star."

After the green star had been fixed to the chart he set one of the boys to read, and when the monotonous drone of his voice was well under way he turned again to span the distance between his high stool and the draper's window. By uniting the figures and faces of the present assistants, and then by dissolving them, he tried to recapture the carnal vision of the girl who had recently died, a practice of reconstruction that had been the mainstay of his sojourn at this school, a line of sight across the cobbled road into Harrison's shop, beamed on to the girls who went to work there when they were fifteen and left at twenty to get married. He had become a connoisseur of young suburban womanhood, and thus the fluctuating labour and marriage market made Mr. Raynor a fickle lover, causing him too often to forget each great passion as another one walked in to take its place. Each 'good' one was credit-starred upon his mind, left behind a trail of memories when it went, until a new 'good' one came like a solid fiscal stamp of spiritual currency that drove the other one out. Each memory was thus renewed, so that none of them died.

But the last one was the best of all, an unexpected beauty back-dropped against the traffic artery of squalid streets. He had watched her work and talk or on wet afternoons stand at the counter as if in a trance. The boy on the front row was reading like a prophet, and an agitated muttering sea began to grow about him, and the curtain of Mr. Raynor's memory drew back upon the runners of a line recalled from Baudelaire: "Timide et libertine, et fragile et robuste"—revealing the secret of her classical beauty and nubility, which vanished when the blood-filled phrase was dragged away by the top deck of a trolley-bus laden with rigid staring faces. A tea-boy carrying a white jug slipped out of the estate agents' offices, dodged deftly through a line of cars and lorries that had stopped for the traffic-lights, and walked whistling a tune into a café further down the road.

The sea of noise surrounding the prophet-like monotonous voice of the reading boy increased to a higher magnitude than discipline would permit, until a wave carried his sonorous words away and another sound dominated the scene. He looked, and saw Bullivant on his feet thumping the boy at the desk in front with all his might. The boy raised his fists to hit back.

Mr. Raynor roared with such fury that there was instant silence, his ageing pink face thrust over his desk towards them. "Come out, Bullivant," he cried. *Libertine et robuste:* the phrase fought and died, was given a white cross and packed away.

Bullivant slouched out between rows of apprehensive boys. "'e 'it me first," he said, nearing the blackboard.

"And now I'm going to hit you," Mr. Raynor retorted, lifting the lid of his desk and taking out a stick. His antagonist eyed him truculently, displaying his contempt of the desperate plight he was supposed to be in by turning around and winking at his friends. He was a big boy of fourteen, wearing long drainpipe trousers and a grey jersey.

"Y'aren't gooin' ter 'it me," he said. "I ain't dun owt ter get 'it, yer know."

"Hold out your hand," Mr. Raynor said, his face turning a deep crimson. *Timide.* No, he thought, not likely. This is the least I can do. I'll get these Teddy-boy ideas out of his head for a few seconds.

No hand was extended towards him as it should have been. Bullivant stood still, and Mr. Raynor repeated his order. The class looked on, and moving traffic on the road hid none of the smaller mutterings that passed for silence. Bullivant still wouldn't lift his hand, and time enough had gone by that could be justified by Mr. Raynor as patience.

"Y'aren't gooin' ter 'it me wi' that," Bullivant said again, a gleam just showing from his blue half-closed eyes.

Robust. An eye for an eye. The body of the girl, the bottom line of the sweater spreading over her hips, was destroyed in silence. His urge for revenge was checked, but was followed by a rage that nevertheless bit hard and forced him to action. In the passing of a bus he stepped to Bullivant's side and struck him several times across the shoulders with the stick, crashing each blow down with all his force. "Take that," he cried out, "you stupid defiant oaf."

Bullivant shied away, and before any more blows could fall, and before Mr. Raynor realized that such a thing was possible, Bullivant lashed back with his fists, and they were locked in a battle of strength, both trying to push the other away, to get clear and strike. Mr. Raynor took up a stance with legs apart, trying to push Bullivant back against the desks, but Bullivant foresaw such a move from his stronger adversary and moved his own body so that they went scuffling between the desks. "Yo' ain't 'ittin' me like that," Bullivant gasped between his teeth. "Oo do yo' think yo' are?" He unscrewed his head that was suddenly beneath Mr. Raynor's arm, threw out his fists that went wide of the mark, and leapt like a giraffe over a row of desks. Mr. Raynor moved quickly and blocked his retreat, grabbed his arm firmly and glowered at him with blood-red face, twisted the captive limb viciously, all in a second, then pushed him free, though he stood with the stick ready in case Bullivant should come for him again.

But Bullivant recognized the dispensation of a truce, and merely said: "I'll bring our big kid up to settle yo'," and sat down. Experience was Mr. Raynor's friend; he saw no point in spinning out trouble to its logical conclusion, which meant only more trouble. He was content to warn Bullivant to behave himself, seeing that no face had been lost by either side in the equal contest. He sat again on the high stool behind his desk. What did it matter, really? Bullivant and most of the others would be leaving in two months, and he could keep them in check for that short time. And after the holidays more Bullivants would move up into his classroom from the scholastic escalator.

It was five minutes to ten, and to ensure that the remaining time was peaceful he took out his Bible and began reading in a clear steady voice:

"Then the Lord said unto Moses (titters here), now shalt thou see what I will do to Pharaoh: for with a strong hand shall he let them go, and with a strong hand shall he drive them out of his land."

The class that came in at half past ten was for arithmetic, and they were told to open their books and do the exercises on page fifty-four. He observed the leaves of many books covered with ink-scrawls, and obscene words written across the illustrations and decorating the 'answer' margins like tattooing on the arms of veteran sailors, pages that would be unrecognizable in a month, but would have to last for another twelve. This was a younger class, whose rebellion had so far reached only the pages of their books.

But that, too, was only something to accept and, inclining his head to the right, he forgot the noise of his class and looked across the road at the girls working in the draper's shop. Oh yes, the last one had been the best he could remember, and the time had come when he decided to cure his madness by speaking to her one evening as she left the shop. It was a good idea. But it was too late, for a young man had begun meeting her and seeing her safely, it seemed, to the bus stop. Most of the girls who gave up their jobs at the shop did so because they met some common fate or other. (*"Timide et libertine, et fragile et robuste"*—he could not forget the phrase.) Some were married, others, he had noticed, became pregnant and disappeared; a few had quarrelled with the manager and appeared to have been sacked. But the last one, he had discovered, on opening the newspaper one evening by the traffic-lights at the corner, had been murdered by the young man who came to meet her.

Three double-decker trolley-buses trundled by in a line, but he still saw her vision by the counter.

"Quiet!" he roared, to the forty faces before him. "The next one to talk gets the stick."

And there was quiet.

The Fishing-boat Picture

I'VE been a postman for twenty-eight years. Take that first sentence: because it's written in a simple way may make the fact of my having been a postman for so long seem important, but I realize that such a fact has no significance whatever. After all, it's not my fault that it may seem as if it has to some people just because I wrote it down plain; I wouldn't know how to do it any other way. If I started using long and complicated words that I'd searched for in the dictionary I'd use them too many times, the same ones over and over again, with only a few sentences—if that—between each one; so I'd rather not make what I'm going to write look foolish by using dictionary words.

It's also twenty-eight years since I got married. That statement is very important no matter how you write it or in what way you look at it. It so happened that I married my wife as soon as I got a permanent job, and the first good one I landed was with the Post Office (before that I'd been errand-boy and mash-lad). I had to marry her as soon as I got a job because I'd promised her I would, and she wasn't the sort of person to let me forget it.

When my first pay night came I called for her and asked: "What about a walk up Snakey Wood?" I was cheeky-daft and on top of the world, and because I'd forgotten about our arrangement I didn't think it strange at all when she said: "Yes, all right." It was late autumn I remember and the leaves were as high as snow, crisp on top but soggy underneath. In the full moon and light wind we walked over the Cherry Orchard, happy and arm-in-arm. Suddenly she stopped and turned to me, a big-boned girl yet with a good figure and a nice enough face: "Do you want to go into the wood?"

What a thing to ask! I laughed: "You know I do. Don't you?"

We walked on, and a minute later she said: "Yes, I do; but you know what we're to do now you've got a steady job, don't you?"

I wondered what it was all about. Yet I knew right enough. "Get married," I admitted, adding on second thoughts: "I don't have much of a wage to be wed on, you know."

"It's enough, as far as I'm concerned," she answered.

And that was that. She gave me the best kiss I'd ever had, and then we went into the wood.

She was never happy about our life together, right from the start. And neither was I, because it didn't take her long to begin telling me that all her friends—her family most of all—said time and time again that our marriage wouldn't last five minutes. I could never say much back to this, knowing after the first few months how right everybody would be. Not that it bothered me though, because I was always the sort of bloke that doesn't get ruffled at anything. If you want to know the truth—the sort of thing I don't suppose many blokes would be ready to admit—the bare fact of my getting married meant only that I changed one house and one mother for another house and a different mother. It was as simple as that. Even my wage-packet didn't alter its course: I handed it over every Friday night and got five shillings back for tobacco and a visit to the pictures. It was the sort of wedding where the cost of the ceremony and reception go as a down payment, and you then continue dishing-out your wages every week for life. Which is where I suppose they got this hire purchase idea from.

But our marriage lasted for more than the five minutes everybody prophesied: it went on for six years; she left me when I was thirty, and when she was thirty-four. The trouble was that when we had a row—and they were rows, swearing, hurling pots: the lot—it was too much like suffering, and in the middle of them it seemed to me as if we'd done nothing but row and suffer like this from the moment we set eyes on each other, with not a moment's break, and that it would go on like this for as long as we stayed together. The truth was, as I see it now—and even saw it sometimes then—that a lot of our time was bloody enjoyable.

I'd had an idea before she went that our time as man and wife was about up, because one day we had the worst fight of them all. We were sitting at home one evening after tea, one at each end of the table, plates empty and bellies full so that there was no excuse for what followed. My head was in a book, and Kathy just sat there.

Suddenly she said: "I do love you, Harry." I didn't hear the words for some time, as is often the case when you're reading a book. Then: "Harry, look at me."

My face came up, smiled, and went down again to my reading. Maybe I was in the wrong, and should have said something, but the book was too good.

"I'm sure all that reading's bad for your eyes," she commented, prising me again from the hot possessive world of India.

"It ain't," I denied, not looking up. She was young and still fair-faced, a passionate loose-limbed thirty-odd that wouldn't let me sidestep either her obstinacy or anger. "My dad used to say that on'y fools read books, because they'd such a lot to learn."

The words hit me and sank in, so that I couldn't resist coming back with, still not looking up: "He on'y said that because he didn't know how to read. He was jealous, if you ask me."

"No need to be jealous of the rammel you stuff your big head with," she said, slowly to make sure I knew she meant every word. The print wouldn't stick any more; the storm was too close.

"Look, why don't *you* get a book, duck?" But she never would, hated them like poison.

She sneered: "I've got more sense; and too much to do."

Then I blew up, in a mild way because I still hoped she wouldn't take on, that I'd be able to finish my chapter. "Well let me read, anyway, wain't you? It's an interesting book, and I'm tired."

But such a plea only gave her another opening. "Tired? You're allus tired." She laughed out loud: "Tired Tim! You ought to do some real work for a change instead of walking the streets with that daft post bag."

I won't go on, spinning it out word for word. In any case not many more passed before she snatched the book out of my hands. "You booky bastard," she screamed, "nowt but books, books, books, you bleddy dead-'ead"—and threw the book on the heaped-up coals, working it further and further into their blazing middle with the poker.

This annoyed me, so I clocked her one, not very hard, but I did. It was a good reading-book, and what's more it belonged to the library. I'd have to pay for a new one. She slammed out of the house, and I didn't see her until next day.

I didn't think to break my heart very much when she skipped off. I'd had enough. All I can say is that it was a stroke of God's luck we never had any kids. She was confined once or twice, but it never came to anything; each time it dragged more bitterness out of her than we could absorb in the few peaceful months that came between. It might have been better if she'd had kids though; you never know.

A month after burning the book she ran off with a house-painter. It was all done very nicely. There was no shouting or knocking each other about or breaking up the happy home. I just came back from work one day and found a note waiting for me. " I am going away and not coming back "—propped on the mantelpiece in front of the clock. No tear stains on the paper, just eight words in pencil on a page of the insurance book—I've still got it in the back of my wallet, though God knows why.

The housepainter she went with had lived in a house on his own, across the terrace. He'd been on the dole for a few months and suddenly got a job at a place twenty miles away I was later told. The neighbours seemed almost eager to let me know —after they'd gone, naturally—that they'd been knocking-on together for about a year. No one knew where they'd skipped off to exactly, probably imagining that I wanted to chase after them. But the idea never occurred to me. In any case what was I to do? Knock him flat and drag Kathy back by the hair? Not likely.

Even now it's no use trying to tell myself that I wasn't disturbed by this change in my life. You miss a woman when she's been living with you in the same house for six years, no matter what sort of cat-and-dog life you led together—though we had our moments, that I will say. After her sudden departure there was something different about the house, about the walls, ceiling and every object in it. And something altered inside me as well—though I tried to tell myself that all was just the same and that Kathy's leaving me wouldn't make a blind bit of difference. Nevertheless time crawled at first, and I felt like a man just learning to pull himself along with a clubfoot; but then the endless evenings of summer came and I was happy almost against my will, too happy anyway to hang on to such torments as sadness and loneliness. The world was moving and, I felt, so was I.

In other words I succeeded in making the best of things, which as much as anything else meant eating a good meal at the canteen every midday. I boiled an egg for breakfast (fried with bacon on Sundays) and had something cold but solid for my tea every night. As things went, it wasn't a bad life. It might have been a bit lonely, but at least it was peaceful, and it got as I didn't mind it, one way or the other. I even lost the feeling of loneliness that had set me thinking a bit too much just after she'd gone. And then I didn't dwell on it any more. I saw enough people on my rounds during the day to last me through the evenings and at week-ends. Sometimes I played draughts at the club, or went out for a slow half pint to the pub up the street.

Things went on like this for ten years. From what I gathered later Kathy had been living in Leicester with her housepainter. Then she came back to Nottingham. She came to see me one Friday evening, payday. From her point of view, as it turned out, she couldn't have come at a better time.

I was leaning on my gate in the backyard smoking a pipe of tobacco. I'd had a busy day on my rounds, an irritating time of it—being handed back letters all along the line, hearing that people had left and that no one had any idea where they'd moved to; and other people taking as much as ten minutes to get out of bed and sign for a registered letter—and now I felt twice as peaceful because I was at home, smoking my pipe in the backyard at the fag-end of an autumn day. The sky was a clear yellow, going green above the housetops and wireless aerials. Chimneys were just beginning to send out evening smoke, and most of the factory motors had been switched off. The noise of kids scooting around lamp-posts and the barking of dogs came from what sounded a long way off. I was about to knock my pipe out, to go back into the house and carry on reading a book about Brazil I'd left off the night before.

As soon as she came around the corner and started walking up the yard I knew her. It gave me a funny feeling, though: ten years ain't enough to change anybody so's you don't recognize them, but it's long enough to make you have to look twice before you're sure. And that split second in between is like a kick in the stomach. She didn't walk with her usual gait, as though she owned the terrace and everybody in it. She was a bit slower than when I'd seen her last, as if she'd bumped into a wall during the last ten years through walking in the cock o' the walk way she'd always had. She didn't seem so sure of herself and was fatter now, wearing a frock left over from the summer and an open winter coat, and her hair had been dyed fair whereas it used to be a nice shade of brown.

I was neither glad nor unhappy to see her, but maybe that's what shock does, because I was surprised, that I will say. Not that I never expected to see her again, but you know how it is, I'd just forgotten her somehow. The longer she was away our married life shrunk to a year, a month, a day, a split second of sparking light I'd met in the black darkness before getting-up time. The memory had drawn itself too far back, even in ten years, to remain as anything much more than a dream. For as soon as I got used to living alone I forgot her.

Even though her walk had altered I still expected her to say something sarky like: "Didn't expect to see me back at the scene of the crime so soon, did you, Harry?" Or: "You thought it wasn't true that a bad penny always turns up again, didn't you?"

But she just stood. "Hello, Harry"—waited for me to lean up off the gate so's she could get in. "It's been a long time since we saw each other, hasn't it?"

I opened the gate, slipping my empty pipe away. "Hello, Kathy," I said, and walked down the yard so that she could come behind me. She buttoned her coat as we went into the kitchen, as though she were leaving the house instead of just going in. "How are you getting on then?" I asked, standing near the fireplace.

Her back was to the wireless, and it didn't seem as if she wanted to look at me. Maybe I was a bit upset after all at her sudden visit, and it's possible I showed it without knowing it at the time, because I filled my pipe up straightaway, a thing I never normally do. I always let one pipe cool down before lighting the next.

"I'm fine," was all she'd say.

"Why don't you sit down then, Kath? I'll get you a bit of a fire soon."

She kept her eyes to herself still, as if not daring to look at the old things around her, which were much as they'd been when she left. However she'd seen enough to remark: "You look after yourself all right."

"What did you expect?" I said, though not in a sarcastic way. She wore lipstick, I noticed, which I'd never seen on her before, and rouge, maybe powder as well, making her look old in a different way, I supposed, than if she'd had nothing on her face at all. It was a thin disguise, yet sufficient to mask from me—and maybe her—the person she'd been ten years ago.

"I hear there's a war coming on," she said, for the sake of talking.

I pulled a chair away from the table. "Come on, sit down, Kathy. Get that weight off your legs"—an old phrase we'd used though I don't know why I brought it out at that moment. "No, I wouldn't be a bit surprised. That bloke Hitler wants a bullet in his brain—like a good many Germans." I looked up and caught her staring at the picture of a fishing boat on the wall: brown and rusty with sails half spread in a bleak sunrise, not far from the beach along which a woman walked bearing a basket of fish on her shoulder. It was one of a set that Kathy's brother had given us as a wedding present, the other two having been smashed up in another argument we'd had. She liked it a lot, this remaining fishing-boat picture. The last of the fleet, we used to call it, in our brighter moments. "How are you getting on?" I wanted to know. "Living all right?"

"All right," she answered. I still couldn't get over the fact that she wasn't as talkative as she had been, that her voice was softer and flatter, with no more bite in it. But perhaps she felt strange at seeing me in the old house again after all this time, with everything just as she'd left it. I had a wireless now, that was the only difference.

"Got a job?" I asked. She seemed afraid to take the chair I'd offered her.

"At Hoskins," she told me, "on Ambergate. The lace factory. It pays forty-two bob a week, which isn't bad." She sat down and did up the remaining button of her coat. I saw she was looking at the fishing-boat picture again. The last of the fleet.

"It ain't good either. They never paid owt but starvation wages and never will I suppose. Where are you living, Kathy?"

Straightening her hair—a trace of grey near the roots—she said: "I've got a house at Sneinton. Little, but it's only seven and six a week. It's noisy as well, but I like it that way. I was always one for a bit of life, you know that. 'A pint of beer and a quart of noise' was what you used to say, didn't you?"

I smiled. "Fancy you remembering that." But she didn't look as though she had much of a life. Her eyes lacked that spark of humour that often soared up into the bonfire of a laugh. The lines around them now served only as an indication of age and passing time. "I'm glad to hear you're taking care of yourself."

She met my eyes for the first time. "You was never very excitable, was you, Harry?"

"No," I replied truthfully, "not all that much."

"You should have been," she said, though in an empty sort of way, "then we might have hit it off a bit better."

"Too late now," I put in, getting the full blow-through of my words. "I was never one for rows and trouble, you know that. Peace is more my line."

She made a joke at which we both laughed. "Like that bloke Chamberlain!"—then moved a plate to the middle of the table and laid her elbows on the cloth. "I've been looking after myself for the last three years."

It may be one of my faults, but I get a bit curious sometimes. "What's happened to that housepainter of yours

then?" I asked this question quite naturally though, because
I didn't feel I had anything to reproach her with. She'd gone
away, and that was that. She hadn't left me in the lurch with
a mountain of debts or any such thing. I'd always let her do
what she liked.

"I see you've got a lot of books," she remarked, noticing one
propped against the sauce bottle, and two more on the
sideboard.

"They pass the time on," I replied, striking a match
because my pipe had gone out. "I like reading."

She didn't say anything for a while. Three minutes I remember, because I was looking across at the clock on the dresser.
The news would have been on the wireless, and I'd missed the
best part of it. It was getting interesting because of the coming
war. I didn't have anything else to do but think this while I
was waiting for her to speak. "He died of lead-poisoning," she
told me. "He did suffer a lot, and he was only forty-two. They
took him away to the hospital a week before he died."

I couldn't say I was sorry, though it was impossible to hold
much against him. I just didn't know the chap. "I don't
think I've got a fag in the place to offer you," I said, looking
on the mantelpiece in case I might find one, though knowing
I wouldn't. She moved when I passed her on my search, scrap-
ing her chair along the floor. "No, don't bother to shift. I
can get by."

"It's all right," she said. "I've got some here"—feeling in
her pocket and bringing out a crumpled five-packet. "Have
one, Harry?"

"No thanks. I haven't smoked a fag in twenty years. You
know that. Don't you remember how I started smoking a
pipe? When we were courting. You gave me one once for my
birthday and told me to start smoking it because it would

make me look more distinguished! So I've smoked one ever since. I got used to it quick enough, and I like it now. I'd never be without it in fact."

As if it were yesterday! But maybe I was talking too much, for she seemed a bit nervous while lighting her fag. I don't know why it was, because she didn't need to be in my house. "You know, Harry," she began, looking at the fishing-boat picture, nodding her head towards it, "I'd like to have that" —as though she'd never wanted anything so much in her life.

"Not a bad picture, is it?" I remember saying. "It's nice to have pictures on the wall, not to look at especially, but they're company. Even when you're not looking at them you know they're there. But you can take it if you like."

"Do you mean that?" she asked, in such a tone that I felt sorry for her for the first time.

"Of course. Take it. I've got no use for it. In any case I can get another picture if I want one, or put a war map up." It was the only picture on that wall, except for the wedding photo on the sideboard below. But I didn't want to remind her of the wedding picture for fear it would bring back memories she didn't like. I hadn't kept it there for sentimental reasons, so perhaps I should have dished it. "Did you have any kids?"

"No," she said, as if not interested. "But I don't like taking your picture, and I'd rather not if you think all that much of it." We sat looking over each other's shoulder for a long time. I wondered what had happened during these ten years to make her talk so sadly about the picture. It was getting dark outside. Why didn't she shut up about it, just take the bloody thing? So I offered it to her again, and to settle the issue unhooked it, dusted the back with a cloth, wrapped it up in brown paper, and tied the parcel with the best post-office string. "There you are," I said, brushing the pots aside, laying it on the table at her elbows.

"You're very good to me, Harry."

"Good! I like that. What does a picture more or less in the house matter? And what does it mean to me, anyway?" I can see now that we were giving each other hard knocks in a way we'd never learned to do when living together. I switched on the electric light. As she seemed uneasy when it showed everything up clearly in the room, I offered to switch it off again.

"No, don't bother"—standing to pick up her parcel. "I think I'll be going now. Happen I'll see you some other time."

"Drop in whenever you feel like it." Why not? We weren't enemies. She undid two buttons of her coat, as though having them loose would make her look more at her ease and happy in her clothes, then waved to me. "So long."

"Good night, Kathy." It struck me that she hadn't smiled or laughed once the whole time she'd been there, so I smiled to her as she turned for the door, and what came back wasn't the bare-faced cheeky grin I once knew, but a wry parting of the lips moving more for exercise than humour. She must have been through it, I thought, and she's above forty now.

So she went. But it didn't take me long to get back to my book.

A few mornings later I was walking up St. Ann's Well Road delivering letters. My round was taking a long time, for I had to stop at almost every shop. It was raining, a fair drizzle, and water rolled off my cape, soaking my trousers below the knees so that I was looking forward to a mug of tea back in the canteen and hoping they'd kept the stove going. If I hadn't been so late on my round I'd have dropped into a café for a cup.

I'd just taken a pack of letters into a grocer's and, coming out, saw the fishing-boat picture in the next-door pawnshop window, the one I'd given Kathy a few days ago. There was no mistaking it, leaning back against ancient spirit-levels, bladeless planes, rusty hammers, trowels, and a violin case with the strap broken. I recognized a chip in the gold-painted woodwork near the bottom left corner of its frame.

For half a minute I couldn't believe it, was unable to make out how it had got there, then saw the first day of my married life and a sideboard loaded with presents, prominent among them this surviving triplet of a picture looking at me from the wreckage of other lives. And here it is, I thought, come down to a bloody nothing. She must have sold it that night before going home, pawnshops always keeping open late on a Friday so that women could get their husbands' suits out of pop for the week-end. Or maybe she'd sold it this morning, and I was only half an hour behind her on my round. Must have been really hard up. Poor Kathy, I thought. Why hadn't she asked me to let her have a bob or two?

I didn't think much about what I was going to do next. I never do, but went inside and stood at the shop counter waiting for a grey-haired doddering skinflint to sort out the popped bundles of two thin-faced women hovering to make sure he knew they were pawning the best of stuff. I was impatient. The place stank of old clothes and mildewed junk after coming out of fresh rain, and besides I was later than ever now on my round. The canteen would be closed before I got back, and I'd miss my morning tea.

The old man shuffled over at last, his hand out. "Got any letters?"

"Nowt like that, feyther. I'd just like to have a look at that picture you've got in your window, the one with a ship on it." The women went out counting what few shillings he'd given them, stuffing pawn-tickets in their purses, and the old man came back carrying the picture as if it was worth five quid.

Shock told me she'd sold it right enough, but belief lagged a long way behind, so I looked at it well to make sure it really was the one. A price marked on the back wasn't plain enough to read. "How much do you want for it?"

"You can have it for four bob."

Generosity itself. But I'm not one for bargaining. I could have got it for less, but I'd rather pay an extra bob than go through five minutes of chinning. So I handed the money over, and said I'd call back for the picture later.

Four measly bob, I said to myself as I sloshed on through the rain. The robbing bastard. He must have given poor Kathy about one and six for it. Three pints of beer for the fishing-boat picture.

I don't know why, but I was expecting her to call again the following week. She came on Thursday, at the same time, and was dressed in the usual way: summer frock showing through her brown winter coat whose buttons she couldn't leave alone, telling me how nervous she was. She'd had a drink or two on her way, and before coming into the house stopped off at the lavatory outside. I'd been late back from work, and hadn't quite finished my tea, asked her if she could do with a cup. "I don't feel like it," came the answer. "I had one not long ago."

I emptied the coal scuttle on the fire. "Sit down nearer the warmth. It's a bit nippy tonight."

She agreed that it was, then looked up at the fishing-boat picture on the wall. I'd been waiting for this, wondered what she'd say when she did, but there was no surprise at seeing it back in the old place, which made me feel a bit disappointed. "I won't be staying long tonight," was all she said. "I've got to see somebody at eight."

Not a word about the picture. "That's all right. How's your work going?"

"Putrid," she answered nonchalantly, as though my question had been out of place. "I got the sack, for telling the forewoman where to get off."

"Oh," I said, getting always to say "Oh" when I wanted to hide my feelings, though it was a safe bet that whenever I did say "Oh" there wasn't much else to come out with.

I had an idea she might want to live in my house again seeing she'd lost her job. If she wanted to she could. And she wouldn't be afraid to ask, even now. But I wasn't going to mention it first. Maybe that was my mistake, though I'll never know. "A pity you got the sack," I put in.

Her eyes were on the picture again, until she asked: "Can you lend me half-a-crown?"

"Of course I can"—emptied my trouser pocket, sorted out half-a-crown, and passed it across to her. Five pints. She couldn't think of anything to say, shuffled her feet to some soundless tune in her mind. "Thanks very much."

"Don't mention it," I said with a smile. I remembered buying a packet of fags in case she'd want one, which shows how much I'd expected her back. "Have a smoke?"—and she took one, struck a match on the sole of her shoe before I could get her a light myself.

"I'll give you the half-crown next week, when I get paid." That's funny, I thought. "I got a job as soon as I lost the

other one," she added, reading my mind before I had time to
speak. "It didn't take long. There's plenty of war work now.
Better money as well."

"I suppose all the firms'll be changing over soon." It
occurred to me that she could claim some sort of allowance
from me—for we were still legally married—instead of coming to borrow half-a-crown. It was her right, and I didn't need
to remind her; I wouldn't be all that much put out if she took
me up on it. I'd been single—as you might say—for so many
years that I hadn't been able to stop myself putting a few
quid by. "I'll be going now," she said, standing up to fasten
her coat.

"Sure you won't have a cup of tea?"

"No thanks. Want to catch the trolley back to Sneinton."
I said I'd show her to the door. "Don't bother. I'll be all
right." She stood waiting for me, looking at the picture on the
wall above the sideboard. "It's a nice picture you've got up
there. I always liked it a lot."

I made the old joke: "Yes, but it's the last of the fleet."

"That's why I like it." Not a word about having sold it
for eighteen pence.

I showed her out, mystified.

She came to see me every week, all through the war, always
on Thursday night at about the same time. We talked a bit,
about the weather, the war, her job and my job, never anything important. Often we'd sit for a long time looking into
the fire from our different stations in the room, me by the
hearth and Kathy a bit further away at the table as if she'd
just finished a meal, both of us silent yet not uneasy in it.
Sometimes I made a cup of tea, sometimes not. I suppose now
that I think of it I could have got a pint of beer in for when

she came, but it never occurred to me. Not that I think she felt the lack of it, for it wasn't the sort of thing she expected to see in my house anyway.

She never missed coming once, even though she often had a cold in the winter and would have been better off in bed. The blackout and shrapnel didn't stop her either. In a quiet off-handed sort of way we got to enjoy ourselves and looked forward to seeing each other again, and maybe they were the best times we ever had together in our lives. They certainly helped us through the long monotonous dead evenings of the war.

She was always dressed in the same brown coat, growing shabbier and shabbier. And she wouldn't leave without borrowing a few shillings. Stood up: " Er . . . lend's half-a-dollar, Harry." Given, sometimes with a joke: " Don't get too drunk on it, will you? "—never responded to, as if it were bad manners to joke about a thing like that. I didn't get anything back of course, but then, I didn't miss such a dole either. So I wouldn't say no when she asked me, and as the price of beer went up she increased the amount to three bob then to three-and-six and, finally, just before she died, to four bob. It was a pleasure to be able to help her. Besides, I told myself, she has no one else. I never asked questions as to where she was living, though she did mention a time or two that it was still up Sneinton way. Neither did I at any time see her outside at a pub or picture house; Nottingham is a big town in many ways.

On every visit she would glance from time to time at the fishing-boat picture, the last of the fleet, hanging on the wall above the sideboard. She often mentioned how beautiful she thought it was, and how I should never part with it, how the sunrise and the ship and the woman and the sea were just right. Then a few minutes later she'd hint to me how nice it would be if she had it, but knowing it would end up in the pawnshop I didn't take her hints. I'd rather have lent her five bob instead of half-a-crown so that she wouldn't take the picture, but she never seemed to want more than half-a-crown in those first years. I once mentioned to her she could have more if she liked, but she didn't answer me. I don't think she wanted the picture especially to sell and get money, or to hang in her own house; only to have the pleasure of pawning it, to have someone else buy it so that it wouldn't belong to either of us any more.

But she finally did ask me directly, and I saw no reason to refuse when she put it like that. Just as I had done six years before, when she first came to see me, I dusted it, wrapped it up carefully in several layers of brown paper, tied it with post-office string, and gave it to her. She seemed happy with it under her arm, couldn't get out of the house quick enough, it seemed.

It was the same old story though, for a few days later I saw it again in the pawnshop window, among all the old junk that had been there for years. This time I didn't go in and try to get it back. In a way I wish I had, because then Kathy might not have had the accident that came a few days later. Though you never know. If it hadn't been that, it would have been something else.

I didn't get to her before she died. She'd been run down by a lorry at six o'clock in the evening, and by the time the police had taken me to the General Hospital she was dead. She'd been knocked all to bits, and had practically bled to death even before they'd got her to the hospital. The doctor told me she'd not been quite sober when she was knocked down. Among the things of hers they showed me was the fishing-boat picture, but it was so broken up and smeared with blood that I hardly recognized it. I burned it in the roaring flames of the firegrate late that night.

When her two brothers, their wives and children had left and taken with them the air of blame they attached to me for Kathy's accident I stood at the graveside thinking I was alone, hoping I would end up crying my eyes out. No such luck. Holding my head up suddenly I noticed a man I hadn't seen before. It was a sunny afternoon of winter, but bitter cold, and the only thing at first able to take my mind off Kathy was the thought of some poor bloke having to break the bone-hard soil and dig this hole she was now lying in. Now there was this stranger. Tears were running down his cheeks, a man in his middle fifties wearing a good suit, grey though but with a black band around his arm, who moved only when the fed-up sexton touched his shoulder—and then mine—to say it was all over.

I felt no need to ask who he was. And I was right. When I got to Kathy's house (it had also been his) he was packing his things, and left a while later in a taxi without saying a word. But the neighbours, who always know everything, told me he and Kathy had been living together for the last six years. Would you believe it? I only wished he'd made her happier than she'd been.

Time has passed now and I haven't bothered to get another picture for the wall. Maybe a war map would do it; the wall gets too blank, for I'm sure some government will oblige soon. But it doesn't really need anything at the moment, to tell you the truth. That part of the room is filled up by the sideboard, on which is still the wedding picture, that she never thought to ask for.

And looking at these few old pictures stacked in the back of my mind I began to realize that I should never have let them go, and that I shouldn't have let Kathy go either. Something told me I'd been daft and dead to do it, and as my rotten luck would have it it was the word dead more than daft that stuck in my mind, and still sticks there like the spinebone of a :od or conger eel, driving me potty sometimes when I lay of a night in bed thinking.

I began to believe there was no point in my life—became even too far gone to turn religious or go on the booze. Why had I lived? I wondered. I can't see anything for it. What was the point of it all? And yet at the worst minutes of my midnight emptiness I'd think less of myself and more of Kathy, see her as suffering in a far rottener way than ever I'd done, and it would come to me—though working only as long as an aspirin pitted against an incurable headache—that the object of my having been alive was that in some small way I'd helped Kathy through her life.

I was born dead, I keep telling myself. Everybody's dead, I answer. So they are, I maintain, but then most of them never know it like I'm beginning to do, and it's a bloody shame that this has come to me at last when I could least do with it, and when it's too bloody late to get anything but bad from it.

Then optimism rides out of the darkness like a knight in armour. If you loved her . . . (of course I bloody-well did) . . . then you both did the only thing possible if it was to be remembered as love. Now didn't you? Knight in armour goes back into blackness. Yes, I cry, but neither of us *did anything about it*, and that's the trouble.

※ʃ※ʃ※ʃ※ʃ※

Noah's Ark

WHILE Jones the teacher unravelled the final
meanderings of *Masterman Ready*, Colin from the
classroom heard another trundle of wagons and
caravans rolling slowly towards the open spaces of the Forest.
His brain was a bottleneck, like the wide boulevard along
which each vehicle passed, and he saw, remembering last year,
fresh-packed ranks of colourful Dodgem Cars, traction engines
and mobile zoos, Ghost Trains and Noah's Ark figures securely
crated on to drays and lorries.

So *Masterman Ready* was beaten by the prospect of more
tangible distraction, though it was rare for a book of dream-
adventures to be banished so easily from Colin's mind. The
sum total of such free-lance wandering took him through bad
days of scarcity, became a mechanical gaudily dressed pied-
piper always ahead, which he would follow and one day scrag
to see what made it tick. How this would come about he didn't
know, didn't even try to find out—while the teacher droned
on with the last few pages of his story.

Though his cousin Bert was eleven—a year older—Colin
was already in a higher class at school, and felt that this
counted for something anyway, even though he had found
himself effortlessly there. With imagination fed by books to
bursting point, he gave little thought to the rags he wore
(except when it was cold) and face paradoxically overfleshed
through lack of food. His hair was too short, even for a three-

penny basin-crop at the barber's—which was the only thing
that bothered him at school in that he was sometimes jocu-
larly referred to as 'Owd Bald-'ead'.

When the Goose Fair came a few pennies had survived his
weekly outlay on comics, but Bert had ways and means of
spinning them far beyond their paltry value. "We'll get
enough money for lots of rides," he said, meeting Colin at the
street corner of a final Saturday. "I'll show you"—putting
his arm around him as they walked up the street.

"How?" Colin wanted to know, protesting: "I'm not
going to rob any shops. I'll tell you that now."

Bert, who had done such things, detected disapproval of his
past, though sensing at the same time and with a certain
pride that Colin would never have the nerve to crack open a
shop at midnight and plug his black hands into huge jars of
virgin sweets. "That's not the only way to get money," he
scoffed. "You only do that when you want summat good. I'll
show you what we'll do when we get there."

Along each misty street they went, aware at every turning
of a low exciting noise from the northern sky. Bellies of cloud
were lighted orange by the fair's reflection, plain for all to see,
an intimidating bully slacking the will and drawing them
towards its heart. "If it's on'y a penny a ride then we've got
two goes each," Colin calculated with bent head, pondering
along the blank flagstoned spaces of the pavement, hands in
pockets pinning down his hard-begotten wealth. He was glad
of its power to take him on to roundabouts, but the thought
of what fourpence would do to the table at home filled him—
when neither spoke—with spasms of deep misery. Fourpence
would buy a loaf of bread or a bottle of milk or some stewing
meat or a pot of jam or a pound of sugar. It would perhaps
stop the agony his mother might be in from seeing his father

black and brooding by the hearth if he—Colin—had handed
the fourpence in for ten Woodbines from the corner shop.
His father would take them with a smile, get up to kiss his
mother in the fussy way he had and mash some tea, a happy
man once more whose re-acquired asset would soon spread to
everyone in the house.

It was marvellous what fourpence would do, if you were
good enough to place it where it rightly belonged—which I'm
not, he thought, because fourpence would also buy a fistful
of comics, or two bars of chocolate or take you twice to the
flea-pit picture-house or give you four rides on Goose Fair,
and the division, the wide dark soil-smelling trench that
parted good from bad was filled with wounds of unhappiness.
And such unhappiness was suspect, because Colin knew that
whistling stone-throwing Bert at his side wouldn't put up
with it for the mere sake of fourpence—no, he'd spend it and
enjoy it, which he was now out to do with half the pennies
Colin had. If Bert robbed a shop or cart he'd take the food
straight home—that much Colin knew—and if he laid his
hands on five bob or a pound he'd give his mother one and six
and say that that was all he'd been able to get doing some sort
of work. But fourpence wouldn't worry him a bit. He'd just
enjoy it. And so would Colin, except in the space of stillness
between roundabouts.

They were close to the fair, walking down the slope of
Bentinck Road, able to distinguish between smells of fish-and-
chips, mussels and brandysnap. "Look on the floor," Bert
called out, ever-sharp and hollow-cheeked with the fire of keeping himself going, lit by an instinct never to starve yet always
looking as if he were starving. The top and back of his head
was padded by overgrown hair, and he slopped along in broken
slippers, hands in pockets, whistling, then swearing black-

and-blue at being swept off the pavement by a tide of youths
and girls.

Colin needed little telling: snapped down to the gutter,
walked a hundred yards doubled-up like a premature rheu-
matic, and later shot straight holding a packet with two whole
cigarettes protruding. "No whacks!" he cried, meaning: No
sharing.

"Come on," Bert said, cajoling, threatening, "don't be
bleedin'-well mingy, our Colin. Let's 'ave one."

Colin stood firm. Finding was keeping. "I'm savin' 'em for
our dad. I don't suppose 'e's got a fag to 'is name."

"Well, my old man ain't never got no fags either, but I
wun't bother to save 'em for 'im if I found any. I mean it
as well."

"P'raps we'll have a drag later on then," Colin conceded,
keeping them in his pocket. They were on the asphalt path
of the Forest, ascending a steep slope. Bert feverishly ripped
open every cast-down packet now, chucking silver paper to
the wind, slipping picture-cards in his pocket for younger
brothers, crushing what remained into a ball and hurling it
towards the darkness where bodies lay huddled together in
some passion that neither of them could understand or even
remotely see the point of.

From the war memorial they viewed the whole fair, a sea
of lights and tent tops flanked on two sides by dimly shaped
houses whose occupants would be happy when the vast
encampment scattered the following week to other towns. A
soughing groan of pleasure was being squeezed out of the
earth, and an occasional crescendo of squeals reached them
from the Swingboats and Big Wheel as though an army were
below, offering human sacrifices before beginning its march.
"Let's get down there," Colin said, impatiently turning over

his pennies. "I want to see things. I want to get on that Noah's Ark."

Sucking penny sticks of brandysnap they pushed by the Ghost Train, hearing girls screaming from its skeleton-filled bowels. "We'll roll pennies on to numbers and win summat," Bert said. "It's easy, you see. All you've got to do is put the pennies on a number when the woman ain't looking." He spoke eagerly, to get Colin's backing in a project that would seem more of an adventure if they were in it together. Not that he was afraid to cheat alone, but suspicion rarely fell so speedily on a pair as it did on a lone boy obviously out for what his hands could pick up. "It's dangerous," Colin argued, though all but convinced, elbowing his way behind. "You'll get copped."

A tall gipsy-looking woman with black hair done up in a ponytail stood in the penny-a-roll stall, queen of its inner circle. She stared emptily before her, though Colin, edging close, sensed how little she missed of movement round about. A stack of coppers crashed regularly from one hand to the other, making a noise which, though not loud, drew attention to the stall—and the woman broke its rhythm now and again to issue with an expression of absolute impartiality a few coins to a nick-hatted man who by controlling two of the wooden slots managed to roll down four pennies at a time. "He ain't winnin', though," Bert whispered in Colin's ear, who saw the truth of it: that he rolled out more than he picked up.

His remark stung through to the man's competing brain. "Who ain't?" he demanded, letting another half-dozen pennies go before swinging round on him.

"Yo' ain't," Bert chelped.

"Ain't I? "—swung-open mac showing egg and beer stains around his buttons.

Bert stood his ground, blue eyes staring. "No, y'ain't."

"That's what yo' think," the man retorted, in spite of everything, even when the woman scooped up more of his pennies.

Bert pointed truculently. "Do you call that winning then? Look at it. I don't." All eyes met on three sad coins lying between squares, and Bert slipped his hand on to the counter where the man had set down a supply-dump of money. Colin watched, couldn't breathe, from fear but also from surprise even though there was nothing about Bert he did not know. A shilling and a sixpence seemed to run into Bert's palm, were straightaway hidden by black fingers curling over them. He reached a couple of pennies with the other hand, but his wrist became solidly clamped against the board. He cried out: "Oo, yer rotten sod. Yer'r 'urtin' me."

The man's eyes, formerly nebulous with beer, now became deep and self-centred with righteous anger. "You should keep your thievin' fingers to yoursen. Come on, you little bogger, drop them pennies."

Colin felt ashamed and hoped he would, wanted to get it over with and lose himself among spinning roundabouts. The black rose of Bert's hand unfolded under pressure, petal by petal, until the coins slid off. "Them's my pennies," he complained. "It's yo' as is the thief, not me. You're a bully as well. I had 'em there ready to roll down as soon as I could get one of them slot things."

"I was looking the other way," said the woman, avoiding trouble; which made the man indignant at getting no help: "Do you think I'm daft then? And blind as well? " he cried.

"You must be," Bert said quietly, "if you're trying to say

I nicked your money." Colin felt obliged to back him up:
"He didn't pinch owt," he said earnestly, exploiting a look
of honesty he could put at will into his face. "I'm not his pal,
mate, but I'll tell you the truth. I was just passin' an' stopped
to look, and he put tuppence down on there, took it from 'is
own pocket."

"You thievin' Radford lot," the man responded angrily,
though freed now from the dead-end of continual losing. "Get
cracking from here, or I'll call a copper."

Bert wouldn't move. "Not till you've gen me my tuppence
back. I worked 'ard for that, at our dad's garden, diggin'
taters up and weedin'." The woman looked vacantly—sending
a column of pennies from one palm to another—beyond them
into packed masses swirling and pushing around her flimsy
island. With face dead-set in dreadful purpose, hat tilted forward and arms all-embracing what money was his, the man
gave in to his fate of being a loser and scooped up all his coins,
though he was struck enough in conscience to leave Bert two
surviving pennies before making off to better luck at another
stall.

"That got shut on 'im," Bert said, his wink at Colin meaning they were one and eightpence to the good.

The riches lasted for an hour, and Colin couldn't remember
having been partner to so much capital, wanted to guard some
from the avid tentacles of the thousand-lighted fair. But it fled
from their itchy fingers—surrendered or captured, it was hard
to say which—spent on shrimps and candyfloss, cakewalk and
helter-skelter. They pushed by sideshow fronts. "You should
have saved some of that dough," Colin said, unable to get used
to being poor again.

"It's no use savin' owt," Bert said. "If you spend it you can
allus get some more"—and became paralysed at the sight of

a half-dressed woman in African costume standing by a pay-
box with a python curled around her buxom top.

Colin argued: "If you save you get money and you can go
away to Australia or China. I want to go to foreign countries.
Eh," he said with a nudge, "it's a wonder that snake don't
bite her, ain't it?"

Bert laughed. "It's the sort that squeezes yer ter death, but
they gi' 'em pills to mek 'em dozy. I want to see foreign
countries as well, but I'll join the army."

"That's no good," Colin said, leading the way to more
roundabouts, "there'll be a war soon, and you might get
killed." Around the base of a Noah's Ark Bert discovered a
tiny door that let them into a space underneath. Colin looked
in, to a deadly midnight noise of grinding machinery. "Where
yer going?"

But Bert was already by the middle, doubled up to avoid
the flying circular up-and-down world rolling round at full
speed above. It seemed to Colin the height of danger—one
blow, or get up without thinking, and you'd be dead, brains
smashed into grey sand, which would put paid to any thoughts
of Australia. Bert though had a cool and accurate sense of
proportion, which drew Colin in despite his fear. He crawled
on hands and knees, until he came level with Bert and roared
into his ear: "What yer looking for?"

"Pennies," Bert screamed back above the din.

They found nothing, retired to a more simple life among
the crowd. Both were hungry, and Colin told himself it must
have been five hours since his four o'clock tea. "I could scoff
a hoss between two mattresses."

"So could I," Bert agreed. "But look what I'm going to
do." A white-scarfed youth wearing a cap, with a girl on his
arm working her way through an outsize candyfloss, emerged

from a gap in the crowd. Colin saw Bert go up to them and say a few words to the youth, who put his hand in his pocket, made a joke that drew a laugh from the girl, and gave something to Bert.

"What yer got?" Colin demanded when he came back.

Ingenious Bert showed him. "A penny. I just went up and said I was hungry and asked 'im for summat."

"I'll try," Colin said, wanting to contribute his share. Bert pulled him back, for the only people available were a middle-aged man and his wife, well-dressed and married. "They wain't gi' yer owt. You want to ask courting couples, or people on their own."

But the man on his own whom Colin asked was argumentative. A penny was a penny. Two and a half cigarettes. "What do you want it for?"

"I'm hungry," was all Colin could say.

A dry laugh. "So am I."

"Well, I'm hungrier. I ain't 'ad a bite t'eat since this morning, honest." The man hesitated, but fetched a handful of coins from his pocket. "You'd better not let a copper see you begging or you'll get sent to Borstal."

Some time later they counted out a dozen pennies. "You don't get nowt unless you ask, as mam allus tells me," Bert grinned. They stood at a tea stall with full cups and a plate of buns, filling themselves to the brim. The near-by Big Wheel spun its passengers towards the clouds, only to spin them down again after a tantalizing glimpse of the whole fair, each descending girl cutting the air with animal screams that made Colin shudder until he realized that they were in no harm, were in fact probably enjoying it. "I feel better now," he said, putting his cup back on the counter.

They walked around caravans backed on to railings at the

Forest edge, looked up steps and into doorways, at bunks and potbellied stoves, at beautiful closed doors painted in many colours and carved with weird designs that mystified Colin and made him think of a visit once made to the Empire. Gipsies, Goose Fair, Theatre—it was all one to him, a heaven-on-earth because together they made up the one slender bridge-head of another world that breached the tall thickets surrounding his own. A connecting link between them was in the wild-eyed children now and again seated on wooden steps; but when Colin went too near for a closer look a child called out in alarm, and a burly adult burst from the caravan and chased them away.

Colin took Bert's arm as they wedged themselves into the solid mass of people, under smoke of food-stalls and traction engines, between lit-up umbrellas and lights on poles. "We've spent all our dough," he said, "and don't have owt left to go on Noah's Ark wi'."

"You don't ev ter worry about that. All yer got ter do is get on and keep moving from one thing to another, follering the man collecting the cash so's he never sees yer or catches up wi' yer. Got me?"

Colin didn't like the sound of it, but went up the Noah's Ark steps, barging through lines of onlookers. "I'll do it first," Bert said. "So keep yer eyes on me and see how it's done. Then yo' can go on."

He first of all straddled a lion. Colin stood by the rail and watched closely. When the Ark began spinning Bert moved discreetly to a cock just behind the attendant who emerged from a hut-like structure in the middle. The roundabout soon took on its fullest speed, until Colin could hardly distinguish one animal from another, and often lost sight of Bert in the quick roaring spin.

Then the world stopped circling, and his turn came: "Are you staying on for a second go?" Bert said no, that it wasn't wise to do it two times on the trot. Colin well knew that it was wrong, and dangerous, which was more to the point, yet when a Noah's Ark stood in your path spinning with the battle honours of its more than human speed-power written on the face of each brief-glimpsed wooden animal, you had by any means to get yourself on to that platform, money or no money, fear or no fear, and stay there through its violent bucking until it stopped. Watching from the outside it seemed that one ride on the glorious Noah's Ark would fill you with similar inexhaustible energy for another year, that at the end of the ride you wouldn't want to come off, would need to stay on for ever until you were either sick or dead with hunger.

He was riding alone, clinging to a tiger on the outer ring of vehicles, slightly sick with apprehension and at the sudden up-and-down motion of starting. He waved to Bert on the first slow time round. Then the roundabout's speed increased and it was necessary to stop hugging the tiger and follow the attendant who had just emerged to begin collecting the fares. But he was afraid, for it seemed that should only one of his fingers relax its hold he would be shot off what was supposed to be a delicious ride and smashed to pieces on hitting the outside rail—or smash anyone else to pieces who happened to be leaning against it.

However with great effort and a sinking heart he leapt: panic jettisoned only in the space between two animals. In this state he almost derailed a near-by couple, and when the man's hand shot out for revenge he felt the wind of a near miss blowing by the side of his face. The vindictive fist continued to ply even when he was securely seated on a zebra so that, faced with more solid danger than empty space, he put his tongue out at the man and let go once more.

He went further forward, still in sight of the attendant's stooping enquiring back. In his confused zig-zag progress— for few animals were now vacant—he worked inward to the centre where it was safer, under a roof of banging drums and cymbals, thinking at one point to wave victoriously to Bert. But the idea slipped over a cliff as he threw himself forward and held on to a horse's tail.

The roundabout could go on faster, judging by shouts and squeals from the girls. Colin's movements were clumsy, and he envied the attendant's dexterity a few yards in front, and admired Bert who had made this same circular Odyssey with so much aplomb. Aware of peril every second he was more fretful now of being shot like a cannonball against wood and iron than being caught by the money-collector. " Bogger this," he cursed. " I don't like it a bit "—laughing grimly and lung- ing out on a downgrade, pegged by even more speed to a double-seated dragon.

A vacant crocodile gave a few seconds enjoyment before he leapt on to an ant-eater to keep his distance equal from the attendant. He thought his round should have finished by now, but suddenly the man turned and began coming back, looking at each rider to be sure they had paid. This was unprecedented. They weren't lax, but once round in one direction was all they ever did—so Bert had assured him—and now here was this sly rotten bastard who'd got the cheek to come round again. That worn't fair.

The soporific, agreeable summer afternoons of *Masterman Ready*, having laid a trap at the back of his mind, caught him for a moment, yet flew away unreal before this real jungle in which he had somehow stumbled. He had to move back now in full view of the attendant, to face a further apprenticeship at taking the roundabout clockwise. It seemed impossible, and in one rash moment he considered making a flying leap into the solid stationary gangway and getting right out of it—for he was certain the man had marked him down, was out to wring his neck before pitching the dead chicken that remained over the heads of the crowd. He glimpsed him, an overalled greasy bastard whose lips clung to a doused-out nub-end, cashbag heavy but feet sure.

How long's this bleeding ride going to go on? he asked himself. It's been an hour already and Bert swore blind it only lasted three minutes. I thought so as well, but I suppose they're making it longer just because that bloke's after me for having cadged a free ride. This jungle was little different from home and street life, yet alarming, more frightening because the speed was exaggerated. His one thought was to abandon the present jungle, hurl himself into the slower with which he was familiar—though in that also he felt a dragging pain that would fling him forth one day.

He went back the same way, almost feeling an affection now on coming against a nuzzle, ear or tail he'd already held on to, going from the sanctuary of ant-eater to dragon to crocodile slowly, then gathering speed and surety in leaping from horse to zebra to tiger and back to lion and cock. No rest for the wicked, his mother always said. But I'm not wicked, he told himself. You'll still get no rest though. I don't want any rest. Not much you don't. Clear-headed now, he was almost running with the roundabout, glancing back when he could—to see the attendant gaining on him—dodging irate fists that lashed out when he missed his grip and smiling at enraged astonished faces as if nothing were the matter, holding on to coat-tail and animal that didn't belong to him.

Things never turn out right, he swore, never, never. Rank-a-tank-a-tank-tank went the music. Clash-ter-clash-ter-clash-clash flew the cymbals, up and down to squeals and shouts, and bump-bump-bump-bumpity-bump went his heart, still audible above everything else, lashing out at the insides of his ears with enormous boxing-gloves, throttling his windpipe with a cloven hoof, stamping on his stomach as though he were a tent from which ten buck-navvies were trying to escape, wanting a pint after a week of thirst.

A hand slid over his shoulder, but with a violent twist he broke free and continued his mad career around the swirling Ark. "He'll get me, he'll get me. He's a man and can run faster than I can. He's had more practice than me." But he lurched and righted himself, spurted forward as if in a race, making such progress that he saw the man's back before him, instead of fleeing from his reaching hand behind. He slowed down too late, for the man, evidently controlled by a wink from the centre, switched back. Colin swivelled also, on the run again.

Compared to what it had been the speed now appeared a snail's pace. The three-minute ride was almost up, but Colin, thinking he would escape, was caught, more securely this time, by neck-scruff and waist. He turned within the grasp, smelling oil and sweat and tobacco, pulling and striking at first then, on an inspired impulse kicking wildly at his ankle, unaware of the pain he was causing because of stabbing aches that spread over his own stubbed toes. The man swore as proficiently as Colin's father when he hit his thumb once putting up shelves in the kitchen. But he was free, and considered that the roundabout up-and-downabout was going slow enough to make a getaway. No need to wait until it really stops, was his last thought.

It was like Buck Rogers landing from a space ship without due care, though a few minutes passed before he was able to think this. Upon leaving the still-swirling platform his body fell into a roll and went out with some force, crashing like a sensitive flesh-and-bone cannonball between a courting couple and piling against the wooden barrier. The ball his body made without him knowing much about it slewed out when he hit the posts, arms and legs flying against the carved and painted woodwork of the balustrade. Clump-clump—in quick succession—but he wasn't aware of any standstill either beyond or behind his soon-opened eyes. The rank-a-tank-tank-tank played him out, a blurring of red-white-and-blue lights and coloured animals, and a feeling of relief once he was away from his pursuer, no matter what peril the reaching of solid earth might surround him with.

Bert had watched the whole three minutes, had tried pushing a way through the crowd to catch Colin as he came off— a small ragged figure elbowing a passage between lounging semi-relaxed legs that nevertheless were not always easy to move, so that he reached him too late. "Come on," he said in a worried voice, "gerrup. I'll give yer a hand. Did yer enjoy your ride?"—trying to make him stand up. Turning to an enquirer: "No, he's my cousin, and he's all right. I can tek care on 'im. Come on, Colin. He's still after you, so let's blow."

Colin's legs were rubber, wanted to stay against the sympathetic hardness of wood. "He slung me off after speeding it up, the rotten sod. It was a dirty trick."

"Come on," Bert urged. "Let's blow town."

"Leave me. I'll crawl. I'll kill him if he comes near me." No spinning now: he felt floorboards, saw legs and the occasional flash of a passing wooden animal. They'd started up again. "It's your turn now, ain't it? " he said angrily to Bert.

No time was lost. Bert bent down and came up with him on his shoulders like an expert gymnast, going white in the face and tottering down the wooden steps, towards warm soil and dust. On the last step he lost his strength, swerved helplessly to the right, and both donkey and burden crashed out of sight by the bottom roundabout boards where no one went.

They lay where they had fallen. "I'm sorry," Bert said. "I didn't know he was looking out for us. And then you go and cop it. A real bastard." His hand was under Colin's armpit to stop him sliding sideways. "Are you all right, though? I wun't a minded if it 'ad bin me, and I mean it. Do you feel sick? Are you going to spew? "—hand clapped over Colin's mouth, that was closed tight anyway. "The snakey bastard, chasing you off like that. He ought to get summonsed, he did an' all."

Colin suddenly stood up, leaned against the boards and, with more confidence in his legs, staggered into the crowd, followed by Bert. Abject and beaten, they walked around until midnight by which time, both dead-tired, the idea occurred to them of going home. "I'll get pasted," Colin said, "because I'm supposed to be in by ten." Bert complained that he was knackered, that he wanted to get back anyway.

Streets around the fair were shrivelling into darkness, took on the hue of cold damp ash. They walked arm-in-arm, inspired enough by empty space to sing loudly a song that Bert's father had taught him:

> "We don't want to charge with the fusiliers
> Bomb with the bombadiers
> Fight for the racketeers
> We want to stay at home!

We want to stay at home!
We want to stay at home! "

words ringing loud and clear out of two gruff voices slop-
ping along on sandalled feet, mouths wide open and arms
on each other's shoulders, turning corners and negotiating
twitchells, singing twice as loud by dead cinema and damp
graveyard:

"We don't want to fight in a Tory war
Die like the lads before
Drown in the mud and gore
We want to go to work. . . ."

swinging along from one verse to another, whose parrot-
fashioned words were less important than the bellows of
steamy breath fogging up cold air always in front of them,
frightening cats and skirting midnight prowlers, and hearing
people tell them to shurrup and let them sleep from angrily
rattled bedroom windows. They stood in the middle of a bigger
road when a car was coming, rock still to test their nerves by
making it stop, then charging off when they had been
successful, to avoid the driver's rage, to reach another corner
and resume locked arms, swinging along to the tune of Rule
Britannia:

"Rule two tanners
Two tanners make a bob,
King George nevernevernever
SHAVES HIS NOB! "

each note wavering on the air, and dying as they turned a

corner; at least it would have sounded like that, if anyone
had been listening to it from the deserted corner before. But
to Colin, the noise stayed, all around their heads and faces,
grinding away the sight and sound of the Noah's Ark jungle
he had ridden on free, and so been pitched from.

On Saturday Afternoon

I ONCE saw a bloke try to kill himself. I'll never forget the day because I was sitting in the house one Saturday afternoon, feeling black and fed-up because everybody in the family had gone to the pictures, except me who'd for some reason been left out of it. 'Course, I didn't know then that I would soon see something you can never see in the same way on the pictures, a real bloke stringing himself up. I was only a kid at the time, so you can imagine how much I enjoyed it.

I've never known a family to look as black as our family when they're fed-up. I've seen the old man with his face so dark and full of murder because he ain't got no fags or was having to use saccharine to sweeten his tea, or even for nothing at all, that I've backed out of the house in case he got up from his fireside chair and came for me. He just sits, almost on top of the fire, his oil-stained Sunday-joint maulers opened out in front of him and facing inwards to each other, his thick shoulders scrunched forward, and his dark brown eyes staring into the fire. Now and again he'd say a dirty word, for no reason at all, the worst word you can think of, and when he starts saying this you know it's time to clear out. If mam's in it gets worse than ever, because she says sharp to him: "What are yo' looking so bleddy black for?" as if it might be because of something she's done, and before you know what's happening he's tipped up a tableful of pots and mam's

gone out of the house crying. Dad hunches back over the fire
and goes on swearing. All because of a packet of fags.

I once saw him broodier than I'd ever seen him, so that I
thought he'd gone crackers in a quiet sort of way—until a fly
flew to within a yard of him. Then his hand shot out, got it,
and slung it crippled into the roaring fire. After that he
cheered up a bit and mashed some tea.

Well, that's where the rest of us get our black looks from.
It stands to reason we'd have them with a dad who carries on
like that, don't it? Black looks run in the family. Some families
have them and some don't. Our family has them right enough,
and that's certain, so when we're fed-up we're really fed-up.
Nobody knows why we get as fed-up as we do or why it gives
us these black looks when we are. Some people get fed-up and
don't look bad at all: they seem happy in a funny sort of
way, as if they've just been set free from clink after being in
there for something they didn't do, or come out of the pictures
after sitting plugged for eight hours at a bad film, or just
missed a bus they ran half a mile for and seen it was the wrong
one just after they'd stopped running—but in our family it's
murder for the others if one of us is fed-up. I've asked myself
lots of times what it is, but I can never get any sort of answer
even if I sit and think for hours, which I must admit I don't
do, though it looks good when I say I do. But I sit and think
for long enough, until mam says to me, at seeing me scrunched
up over the fire like dad: "What are yo' looking so black
for?" So I've just got to stop thinking about it in case I get
really black and fed-up and go the same way as dad, tipping
up a tableful of pots and all.

Mostly I suppose there's nothing to look so black for:
though it's nobody's fault and you can't blame anyone for
looking black because I'm sure it's summat in the blood. But

on this Saturday afternoon I was looking so black that when dad came in from the bookie's he said to me: "What's up wi' yo'?"

"I feel badly," I fibbed. He'd have had a fit if I'd said I was only black because I hadn't gone to the pictures.

"Well have a wash," he told me.

"I don't want a wash," I said, and that was a fact.

"Well, get outside and get some fresh air then," he shouted.

I did as I was told, double-quick, because if ever dad goes as far as to tell me to get some fresh air I know it's time to get away from him. But outside the air wasn't so fresh, what with that bloody great bike factory bashing away at the yard-end. I didn't know where to go, so I walked up the yard a bit and sat down near somebody's back gate.

Then I saw this bloke who hadn't lived long in our yard. He was tall and thin and had a face like a parson except that he wore a flat cap and had a moustache that drooped, and looked as though he hadn't had a square meal for a year. I didn't think much o' this at the time: but I remember that as he turned in by the yard-end one of the nosy gossiping women who stood there every minute of the day except when she trudged to the pawnshop with her husband's bike or best suit, shouted to him: "What's that rope for, mate?"

He called back: "It's to 'ang messen wi', missis," and she cackled at his bloody good joke so loud and long you'd think she never heard such a good 'un, though the next day she cackled on the other side of her fat face.

He walked by me puffing a fag and carrying his coil of brand-new rope, and he had to step over me to get past. His boot nearly took my shoulder off, and when I told him to watch where he was going I don't think he heard me because he didn't even look round. Hardly anybody was about. All the kids were still at the pictures, and most of their mams and dads were downtown doing the shopping.

The bloke walked down the yard to his back door, and having nothing better to do because I hadn't gone to the pictures I followed him. You see, he left his back door open a bit, so I gave it a push and went in. I stood there, just watching him, sucking my thumb, the other hand in my pocket. I suppose he knew I was there, because his eyes were moving more natural now, but he didn't seem to mind. "What are yer going to do wi' that rope, mate? " I asked him.

"I'm going ter 'ang messen, lad," he told me, as though he'd done it a time or two already, and people had usually asked him questions like this beforehand.

"What for, mate? " He must have thought I was a nosy young bogger.

" 'Cause I want to, that's what for," he said, clearing all the pots off the table and pulling it to the middle of the room. Then he stood on it to fasten the rope to the light-fitting. The table creaked and didn't look very safe, but it did him for what he wanted.

"It wain't hold up, mate," I said to him, thinking how much better it was being here than sitting in the pictures and seeing the Jungle Jim serial.

But he got nettled now and turned on me. "Mind yer own business."

I thought he was going to tell me to scram, but he didn't. He made ever such a fancy knot with that rope, as though he'd been a sailor or summat, and as he tied it he was whistling a fancy tune to himself. Then he got down from the table and pushed it back to the wall, and put a chair in its place. He wasn't looking black at all, nowhere near as black as anybody in our family when they're feeling fed-up. If ever he'd looked only half as black as our dad looked twice a week he'd have hanged himself years ago, I couldn't help thinking. But he was making a good job of that rope all right, as though he'd thought about it a lot anyway, and as though it was going to be the last thing he'd ever do. But I knew something he didn't know, because he wasn't standing where I was. I knew the rope wouldn't hold up, and I told him so, again.

"Shut yer gob," he said, but quiet like, "or I'll kick yer out."

I didn't want to miss it, so I said nothing. He took his cap off and put it on the dresser, then he took his coat off, and his scarf, and spread them out on the sofa. I wasn't a bit frightened, like I might be now at sixteen, because it was interesting. And being only ten I'd never had a chance to see a bloke hang himself before. We got pally, the two of us, before he slipped the rope around his neck.

"Shut the door," he asked me, and I did as I was told. "Ye're a good lad for your age," he said to me while I sucked my thumb, and he felt in his pockets and pulled out all that was inside, throwing the handful of bits and bobs on the table: fag-packet and peppermints, a pawn-ticket, an old comb, and a few coppers. He picked out a penny and gave it to me, saying: "Now listen ter me, young 'un. I'm going to 'ang messen, and when I'm swinging I want you to gi' this chair a bloody good kick and push it away. All right?"

I nodded.

He put the rope around his neck, and then took it off like it was a tie that didn't fit. "What are yer going to do it for, mate?" I asked again.

"Because I'm fed-up," he said, looking very unhappy. "And because I want to. My missus left me, and I'm out o' work."

I didn't want to argue, because the way he said it, I knew he couldn't do anything else except hang himself. Also there was a funny look in his face: even when he talked to me I swear he couldn't see me. It was different to the black looks my old man puts on, and I suppose that's why my old man would never hang himself, worse luck, because he never gets a look into his clock like this bloke had. My old man's look stares *at* you, so that you have to back down and fly out of the house: this bloke's look looked *through* you, so that you could face it and know it wouldn't do you any harm. So I saw now that dad would never hang himself because he could never get the right sort of look into his face, in spite of the fact that he'd been out of work often enough. Maybe mam would have to leave him first, and then he might do it; but no—I shook my head—there wasn't much chance of that even though he did lead her a dog's life.

"Yer wain't forget to kick that chair away?" he reminded me, and I swung my head to say I wouldn't. So my eyes were popping and I watched every move he made. He stood on the chair and put the rope around his neck so that it fitted this time, still whistling his fancy tune. I wanted to get a better goz at the knot, because my pal was in the scouts, and would ask to know how it was done, and if I told him later he'd let me know what happened at the pictures in the Jungle Jim serial, so's I could have my cake and eat it as well, as mam says, tit for tat. But I thought I'd better not ask the bloke to tell me, and I stayed back in my corner. The last thing he did was take the wet dirty butt-end from his lips and sling it into the empty firegrate, following it with his eyes to the black fireback where it landed—as if he was then going to mend a fault in the lighting like any electrician.

Suddenly his long legs wriggled and his feet tried to kick the chair, so I helped him as I'd promised I would and took a runner at it as if I was playing centre-forward for Notts Forest, and the chair went scooting back against the sofa, dragging his muffler to the floor as it tipped over. He swung for a bit, his arms chafing like he was a scarecrow flapping birds away, and he made a noise in his throat as if he'd just took a dose of salts and was trying to make them stay down.

Then there was another sound, and I looked up and saw a big crack come in the ceiling, like you see on the pictures when an earthquake's happening, and the bulb began circling round and round as though it was a space ship. I was just beginning to get dizzy when, thank Christ, he fell down with such a horrible thump on the floor that I thought he'd broke every bone he'd got. He kicked around for a bit, like a dog that's got colic bad. Then he lay still.

I didn't stay to look at him. "I told him that rope wouldn't hold up," I kept saying to myself as I went out of the house, tut-tutting because he hadn't done the job right, hands stuffed deep into my pockets and nearly crying at the balls-up he'd made of everything. I slammed his gate so hard with disappointment that it nearly dropped off its hinges.

Just as I was going back up the yard to get my tea at home, hoping the others had come back from the pictures so's I wouldn't have anything to keep on being black about, a copper passed me and headed for the bloke's door. He was striding quickly with his head bent forward, and I knew that somebody had narked. They must have seen him buy the rope and then tipped-off the cop. Or happen the old hen at the yard-end had finally caught on. Or perhaps he'd even told somebody himself, because I supposed that the bloke who'd strung himself up hadn't much known what he was doing, especially with the look I'd seen in his eyes. But that's how it is, I said to myself, as I followed the copper back to the bloke's house, a poor bloke can't even hang himself these days.

When I got back the copper was slitting the rope from his neck with a pen-knife, then he gave him a drink of water, and the bloke opened his peepers. I didn't like the copper, because he'd got a couple of my mates sent to approved school for pinching lead piping from lavatories.

"What did you want to hang yourself for?" he asked the bloke, trying to make him sit up. He could hardly talk, and one of his hands was bleeding from where the light-bulb had smashed. I knew that rope wouldn't hold up, but he hadn't listened to me. I'll never hang myself anyway, but if I want to I'll make sure I do it from a tree or something like that, not a light fitting. "Well, what did you do it for?"

"Because I wanted to," the bloke croaked.

"You'll get five years for this," the copper told him. I'd crept back into the house and was sucking my thumb in the same corner.

"That's what yo' think," the bloke said, a normal frightened look in his eyes now. "I only wanted to hang myself."

"Well," the copper said, taking out his book, "it's against the law, you know."

"Nay," the bloke said, "it can't be. It's my life, ain't it?"

"You might think so," the copper said, "but it ain't."

He began to suck the blood from his hand. It was such a little scratch though that you couldn't see it. "That's the first thing I knew," he said.

"Well I'm telling you," the copper told him.

'Course, I didn't let on to the copper that I'd helped the bloke to hang himself. I wasn't born yesterday, nor the day before yesterday either.

"It's a fine thing if a bloke can't tek his own life," the bloke said, seeing he was in for it.

"Well he can't," the copper said, as if reading out of his book and enjoying it. "It ain't your life. And it's a crime to take your own life. It's killing yourself. It's suicide."

The bloke looked hard, as if every one of the copper's words meant six-months cold. I felt sorry for him, and that's a fact, but if only he'd listened to what I'd said and not depended on that light-fitting. He should have done it from a tree, or something like that.

He went up the yard with the copper like a peaceful lamb, and we all thought that that was the end of that.

But a couple of days later the news was flashed through to us—even before it got to the *Post* because a woman in our yard worked at the hospital of an evening dishing grub out and tidying up. I heard her spilling it to somebody at the yard-end. "I'd never 'ave thought it. I thought he'd got that daft idea out of his head when they took him away. But no. Wonders'll never cease. Chucked 'issen from the hospital window when the copper who sat near his bed went off for a pee. Would you believe it? Dead? Not much 'e ain't."

He'd heaved himself at the glass, and fallen like a stone on to the road. In one way I was sorry he'd done it, but in another I was glad, because he'd proved to the coppers and everybody whether it was his life or not all right. It was marvellous though, the way the brainless bastards had put him in a ward six floors up, which finished him off, proper, even better than a tree.

All of which will make me think twice about how black I sometimes feel. The black coal-bag locked inside you, and the black look it puts on your face, doesn't mean you're going to string yourself up or sling yourself under a double-decker

or chuck yourself out of a window or cut your throat with a
sardine-tin or put your head in the gas-oven or drop your
rotten sack-bag of a body on to a railway line, because when
you're feeling that black you can't even move from your chair.
Anyhow, I know I'll never get so black as to hang myself,
because hanging don't look very nice to me, and never will,
the more I remember old what's-his-name swinging from the
light-fitting.

More than anything else, I'm glad now I didn't go to the
pictures that Saturday afternoon when I was feeling black
and ready to do myself in. Because you know, I shan't ever
kill myself. Trust me. I'll stay alive half-barmy till I'm a
hundred and five, and then go out screaming blue murder
because I want to stay where I am.

The Match

B RISTOL CITY had played Notts County and won. Right from the kick-off Lennox had somehow known that Notts was going to lose, not through any pro-phetic knowledge of each home-player's performance, but because he himself, a spectator, hadn't been feeling in top form. One-track pessimism had made him godly enough to inform his mechanic friend Fred Iremonger who stood by his side: "I knew they'd bleddy-well lose, all the time."

Towards the end of the match, when Bristol scored their winning goal, the players could only just be seen, and the ball was a roll of mist being kicked about the field. Advertising boards above the stands, telling of pork-pies, ales, whisky, cigarettes and other delights of Saturday night, faded with the afternoon visibility.

They stood in the one-and-threes, Lennox trying to fix his eyes on the ball, to follow each one of its erratic well-kicked movements, but after ten minutes going from blurred player to player he gave it up and turned to look at the spectators massed in the rising stands that reached out in a wide arc on either side and joined dimly way out over the pitch. This prov-ing equally futile he rubbed a clenched hand into his weak eyes and squeezed them tight, as if pain would give them more strength. Useless. All it produced was a mass of grey squares dancing before his open lids, so that when they cleared his sight was no better than before. Such an affliction

made him appear more phlegmatic at a football match than
Fred and most of the others round about, who spun rattles,
waved hats and scarves, opened their throats wide to each
fresh vaccillation in the game.

During his temporary blindness the Notts' forwards were
pecking and weaving around the Bristol goal and a bright slam
from one of them gave rise to a false alarm, an indecisive
rolling of cheers roofed in by a grey heavy sky. " What's up? "
Lennox asked Fred. " Who scored? Anybody? "

Fred was a younger man, recently married, done up in his
Saturday afternoon best of sports coat, gaberdine trousers and
rain-mac, dark hair sleeked back with oil. " Not in a month
of Sundays," he laughed, "but they had a bleddy good try,
I'll tell you that."

By the time Lennox had focused his eyes once more on the
players the battle had moved to Notts' goal and Bristol were
about to score. He saw a player running down the field, hearing in his imagination the thud of boots on damp introdden
turf. A knot of adversaries dribbled out in a line and straggled
behind him at a trot. Suddenly the man with the ball spurted
forward, was seen to be clear of everyone as if, in a second of
time that hadn't existed to any spectator or other player, he'd
been catapulted into a hallowed untouchable area before the
goal posts. Lennox's heart stopped beating. He peered between
two oaken unmovable shoulders that, he thought with anger,
had swayed in front purposely to stop him seeing. The rene-
gade centre-forward from the opposing side was seen, like a
puppet worked by someone above the low clouds, to bring his
leg back, lunge out heavily with his booted foot. " No," Lennox had time to say. " Get on to him you dozy sods. Don't let
him get it in."

From being an animal pacing within the prescribed area of

his defended posts, the goalkeeper turned into a leaping ape, arms and legs outstretched, then became a mere stick that swung into a curve—and missed the ball as it sped to one side and lost itself in folds of net behind him.

The lull in the general noise seemed like silence for the mass of people packed about the field. Everyone had settled it in his mind that the match, as bad as it was, would be a draw, but now it was clear that Notts, the home team, had lost. A great roar of disappointment and joy, from the thirty thousand spectators who hadn't realized that the star of Bristol City was so close, or who had expected a miracle from their own stars at the last moment, ran up the packed embankments, overflowing into streets outside where groups of people, startled at the sudden noise of an erupting mob, speculated as to which team had scored.

Fred was laughing wildly, jumping up and down, bellowing something between a cheer and a shout of hilarious anger, as if out to get his money's worth on the principle that an adverse goal was better than no goal at all. " Would you believe it? " he called at Lennox. " Would you believe it? Ninety-five thousand quid gone up like Scotch mist ! "

Hardly knowing what he was doing Lennox pulled out a cigarette, lit it. " It's no good," he cursed, " they've lost. They should have walked away with the game "—adding under his breath that he must get some glasses in order to see things better. His sight was now so bad that the line of each eye crossed and converged some distance in front of him. At the cinema he was forced down to the front row, and he was never the first to recognize a pal on the street. And it spelt ruination for any football match. He could remember being able to pinpoint each player's face, and distinguish every spectator around the field, yet he still persuaded himself that he had no

need of glasses and that somehow his sight would begin to
improve. A more barbed occurrence connected with such eyes
was that people were beginning to call him Cock-eye. At the
garage where he worked the men sat down to tea-break the
other day, and because he wasn't in the room one of them
said: "Where's owd Cock-eye? 'Is tea'll get cold."

"What hard lines," Fred shouted, as if no one yet knew
about the goal. "Would you believe it?" The cheering and
booing were beginning to die down.

"That goalie's a bloody fool," Lennox swore, cap pulled
low over his forehead. "He couldn't even catch a bleeding
cold."

"It was dead lucky," Fred put in reluctantly, "they
deserved it, I suppose"—simmering down now, the full force
of the tragedy seeping through even to his newly wedded body
and soul. "Christ, I should have stayed at home with my
missis. I'd a bin warm there, I know that much. I might even
have cut myself a chunk of hearthrug pie if I'd have asked
her right!"

The laugh and wink were intended for Lennox, who was
still in the backwater of his personal defeat. "I suppose that's
all you think on these days," he said wryly.

"'Appen I do, but I don't get all that much of it, I can tell
you." It was obvious though that he got enough to keep him
in good spirits at a cold and disappointing football match.

"Well," Lennox pronounced, "all that'll alter in a bit.
You can bet on that."

"Not if I know it," Fred said with a broad smile. "And I
reckon it's better after a bad match than if I didn't come to
one."

"You never said a truer word about bad," Lennox said. He
bit his lip with anger. "Bloody team. They'd even lose at blow

football." A woman behind, swathed in a thick woollen scarf coloured white and black like the Notts players, who had been screaming herself hoarse in support of the home team all the afternoon was almost in tears at the adverse goal. "Foul! Foul! Get the dirty lot off the field. Send 'em back to Bristol where they came from. Foul! Foul I tell yer."

People all around were stamping feet dead from the cold, having for more than an hour staved off its encroachment into their limbs by the hope of at least one home-team win before Christmas. Lennox could hardly feel his, hadn't the will to help them back to life, especially in face of an added force to the bitter wind, and a goal that had been given away so easily. Movement on the pitch was now desultory, for there were only ten minutes of play left to go. The two teams knotted up towards one goal, then spread out around an invisible ball, and moved down the field again, back to the other with no decisive result. It seemed that both teams had accepted the present score to be the final state of the game, as though all effort had deserted their limbs and lungs.

"They're done for," Lennox observed to Fred. People began leaving the ground, making a way between those who were determined to see the game out to its bitter end. Right up to the dull warbling blast of the final whistle the hard core of optimists hoped for a miraculous revival in the worn-out players.

"I'm ready when yo' are," Fred said.

"Suits me." He threw his cigarette-end to the floor and, with a grimace of disappointment and disgust, made his way up the steps. At the highest point he turned a last glance over the field, saw two players running and the rest standing around in deepening mist—nothing doing—so went on down towards the barriers. When they were on the road a great cheer rose behind, as a whistle blew the signal for a mass rush to follow.

Lamps were already lit along the road, and bus queues grew quickly in semi-darkness. Fastening up his mac Lennox hurried across the road. Fred lagged behind, dodged a trolley-bus that sloped up to the pavement edge like a man-eating monster and carried off a crowd of people to the city-centre with blue lights flickering from overhead wires. "Well," Lennox said when they came close, "after that little lot I only hope the wife's got summat nice for my tea."

"I can think of more than that to hope for," Fred said. "I'm not one to grumble about my grub."

"'Course," Lennox sneered, "you're living on love. If you had Kit-E-Kat shoved in front of you you'd say it was a good dinner." They turned off by the recruiting centre into the heart of the Meadows, an ageing suburb of black houses and small factories. "That's what yo' think," Fred retorted, slightly offended yet too full of hope to really mind. "I'm just not one to grumble a lot about my snap, that's all."

"It wouldn't be any good if you was," Lennox rejoined, "but the grub's rotten these days, that's the trouble. Either frozen, or in tins. Nowt natural. The bread's enough to choke yer." And so was the fog: weighed down by frost it lingered and thickened, causing Fred to pull up his rain-mac collar. A man who came level with them on the same side called out derisively: "Did you ever see such a game?"

"Never in all my born days," Fred replied.

"It's always the same though," Lennox was glad to comment, "the best players are never on the field. I don't know what they pay 'em for."

The man laughed at this sound logic. "They'll 'appen get 'em on nex' wik. That'll show 'em."

"Let's hope so," Lennox called out as the man was lost in the fog. "It ain't a bad team," he added to Fred. But that wasn't what he was thinking. He remembered how he had been up before the gaffer yesterday at the garage for clouting the mash-lad who had called him Cock-eye in front of the office-girl, and the manager said that if it happened again he would get his cards. And now he wasn't sure that he wouldn't ask for them anyway. He'd never lack a job, he told himself, knowing his own worth and the sureness of his instinct when dissecting piston from cylinder, camshaft and connecting-rod and searching among a thousand-and-one possible faults before setting an engine bursting once more with life. A small boy called from the doorway of a house: "What's the score, mate?"

"They lost, two-one," he said curtly, and heard a loud clear-sounding doorslam as the boy ran in with the news. He walked with hands in pockets, and a cigarette at the corner of his mouth so that ash occasionally fell on to his mac. The smell of fish-and-chips came from a well-lit shop, making him feel hungry.

"No pictures for me tonight," Fred was saying. "I know the best place in weather like this." The Meadows were hollow with the clatter of boots behind them, the muttering of voices hot in discussion about the lost match. Groups gathered at each corner, arguing and teasing any girl that passed, lighted gas-lamps a weakening ally in the fog. Lennox turned into an entry, where the cold damp smell of backyards mingled with that of dustbins. They pushed open gates to their separate houses.

"So long. See you tomorrow at the pub maybe."

"Not tomorrow," Fred answered, already at his back door. "I'll have a job on mending my bike. I'm going to gi' it a coat of enamel and fix in some new brake blocks. I nearly got flattened by a bus the other day when they didn't work."

The gate-latch clattered. "All right then," Lennox said, "see you soon"—opening the back door and going into his house.

He walked through the small living-room without speaking, took off his mac in the parlour. "You should mek a fire in there," he said, coming out. "It smells musty. No wonder the clo'es go to pieces inside six months." His wife sat by the fire knitting from two balls of electric-blue wool in her lap. She was forty, the same age as Lennox, but gone to a plainness and discontented fat, while he had stayed thin and wiry from the same reason. Three children, the eldest a girl of fourteen, were at the table finishing tea.

Mrs. Lennox went on knitting. "I was going to make one today but I didn't have time."

"Iris can mek one," Lennox said, sitting down at the table.

The girl looked up. "I haven't finished my tea yet, our dad." The wheedling tone of her voice made him angry. "Finish it later," he said with a threatening look. "The fire needs making now, so come on, look sharp and get some coal from the cellar."

She didn't move, sat there with the obstinacy of the young spoiled by a mother. Lennox stood up. "Don't let me have to tell you again." Tears came into her eyes. "Go on," he shouted. "Do as you're told." He ignored his wife's plea to stop picking on her and lifted his hand to settle her with a blow.

"All right, I'm going. Look"—she got up and went to the cellar door. So he sat down again, his eyes roaming over the well-set table before him, holding his hands tightly clenched beneath the cloth. "What's for tea, then?"

His wife looked up again from her knitting. "There's two kippers in the oven."

He did not move, sat morosely fingering a knife and fork, "Well?" he demanded. "Do I have to wait all night for a bit o' summat t'eat?"

Quietly she took a plate from the oven and put it before him. Two brown kippers lay steaming across it. "One of these days," he said, pulling a long strip of white flesh from the bone, "we'll have a change."

"That's the best I can do," she said, her deliberate patience no way to stop his grumbling—though she didn't know what else would. And the fact that he detected it made things worse.

"I'm sure it is," he retorted. The coal bucket clattered from the parlour where the girl was making a fire. Slowly, he picked his kippers to pieces without eating any. The other two children sat on the sofa watching him, not daring to talk. On one side of his plate he laid bones; on the other, flesh. When the cat rubbed against his leg he dropped pieces of fish for it on to the lino, and when he considered that it had eaten enough he kicked it away with such force that its head knocked against the sideboard. It leapt on to a chair and began to lick itself, looking at him with green surprised eyes.

He gave one of the boys sixpence to fetch a *Football Guardian*. "And be quick about it," he called after him. He pushed his plate away, and nodded towards the mauled kippers. "I don't want this. You'd better send somebody out for some pastries. And mash some fresh tea," he added as an afterthought, "that pot's stewed."

He had gone too far. Why did he make Saturday afternoon such hell on earth? Anger throbbed violently in her temples. Through the furious beating of her heart she cried out: "If you want some pastries you'll fetch 'em yourself. And you'll mash your own tea as well."

"When a man goes to wok all week he wants some tea," he said, glaring at her. Nodding at the boy: "Send him out for some cakes."

The boy had already stood up. "Don't go. Sit down," she said to him. "Get 'em yourself," she retorted to her husband. "The tea I've already put on the table's good enough for anybody. There's nowt wrong wi' it at all, and then you carry on like this. I suppose they lost at the match, because I can't think of any other reason why you should have such a long face."

He was shocked by such a sustained tirade, stood up to subdue her. "You what?" he shouted. "What do you think you're on wi'?"

Her face turned a deep pink. "You heard," she called back. "A few home truths might do you a bit of good."

He picked up the plate of fish and, with exaggerated deliberation, threw it to the floor. "There," he roared. "That's what you can do with your bleeding tea."

"You're a lunatic," she screamed. "You're mental."

He hit her once, twice, three times across the head, and knocked her to the ground. The little boy wailed, and his sister came running in from the parlour. . . .

Fred and his young wife in the house next door heard a commotion through the thin walls. They caught the cadence of voices and shifting chairs, but didn't really think anything amiss until the shriller climax was reached. "Would you believe it?" Ruby said, slipping off Fred's knee and straightening her skirt. "Just because Notts have lost again. I'm glad yo' aren't like that."

Ruby was nineteen, plump like a pear not round like a pudding, already pregnant though they'd only been married a month. Fred held her back by the waist. "I'm not so daft as to let owt like that bother me."

She wrenched herself free. "It's a good job you're not; because if you was I'd bosh you one."

Fred sat by the fire with a bemused, Cheshire-cat grin on his face while Ruby was in the scullery getting them something to eat. The noise in the next house had died down. After a slamming of doors and much walking to and fro outside Lennox's wife had taken the children, and left him for the last time.

The Disgrace of Jim Scarfedale

I'M easily led and swung, my mind like a weather-vane when somebody wants to change it for me, but there's one sure rule I'll stick to for good, and I don't mind driving a nail head-first into a bloody long rigmarole of a story to tell you what I mean.

Jim Scarfedale.

I'll never let anybody try and tell me that you don't have to sling your hook as soon as you get to the age of fifteen. You ought to be able to do it earlier, only it's against the law, like everyone else in this poxetten land of hope and glory.

You see, you can't hang on to your mam's apron strings for ever, though it's a dead cert there's many a bloke as would like to. Jim Scarfedale was one of these. He hung on so long that in the end he couldn't get used to anything else, and when he tried to change I swear blind he didn't know the difference between an apron string and a pair of garters, though I'm sure his brand-new almost-beautiful wife must have tried to drum it into his skull before she sent him whining back to his mother.

Well, I'm not going to be one of that sort. As soon as I see a way of making-off—even if I have to rob meters to feed myself—I'll take it. Instead of doing arithmetic lessons at school I glue my eyes to the atlas under my desk, planning the way I'm going to take when the time comes (with the

ripped-out map folded-up in my back pocket): bike to Derby,
bus to Manchester, train to Glasgow, nicked car to Edinburgh,
and hitch-hiking down to London. I can never stop looking at
them maps, with their red roads and brown hills and marvellous other cities—so it's no wonder I can't add up for toffee.
(Yes, I know, every city's the same when you come to weigh
it up: the same hostels full of thieves all out to snatch your
last bob if you give them half the chance; the same factories
full of work, if you're lucky; the same mildewed backyards
and houses full of silverfish and black-clocks when you suddenly switch on the light at night; but nevertheless, even
though they're all the same they're different as well in dozens
of ways, and nobody can deny it.)

Jim Scarfedale lived in our terrace, with his mam, in a
house like our own, only it was a lot nearer the bike factory,
smack next to it in fact, so that it was a marvel to me how
they stuck it with all the noise you could hear. They might
just as well have been inside the factory, because the racket
it kicked up was killing. I went in the house once to tell Mrs.
Scarfedale that Mr. Taylor at the shop wanted to see her
about her week's grub order, and while I was telling her this
I could hear the engines and pulleys next door in the factory
thumping away, and iron-presses slamming as if they were
trying to burst through the wall and set up another department at the Scarfedales'. It wouldn't surprise me a bit if it
was this noise, as much as Jim's mam, that made him go the
way he did.

Jim's mam was a big woman, a Tartar, a real six-footer who
kept her house as clean as a new pin, and who fed Jim up to
his eyeballs on steam puddings and Irish stew. She was the
sort of woman as 'had a way with her'—which meant that

she usually got what she wanted and knew that what she wanted was right. Her husband had coughed himself to death with consumption not long after Jim was born, and Mrs. Scarfedale had set to working at the tobacco factory to earn enough for herself and Jim. She stayed hard at it for donkey's years, and she had a struggle to make ends meet through the dole days, I will say that for her, and Jim always had some sort of suit on his back every Sunday morning—which was a bloody sight more than anybody else in the terrace had. But even though he was fed more snap than the rest of us he was a small lad, and I was as big at thirteen as he was at twenty-seven (by which time it struck me that he must have stopped growing) even though I'd been half clambed to death. The war was on then—when we in our family thought we were living in the lap of luxury because we were able to stuff ourselves on date-jam and oxo—and they didn't take Jim in the army because of his bad eyes, and his mam was glad at this because his dad had got a gob full of gas in the Great War. So Jim stayed with his mam, which I think was worse in the end than if he'd gone for a soldier and been blown to bits by the Jerries.

It worn't long after the war started that Jim surprised us all by getting married.

When he told his mam what he was going to do there was such ructions that we could hear them all the way up the yard. His mam hadn't even seen the girl, and that was what made it worse, she shouted. Courting on the sly like that and suddenly upping and saying he was getting married, without having mentioned a word of it before. Ungrateful, after all she'd done for him, bringing him up so well, even though he'd had no dad. Think of all the times she'd slaved for him! Think of it! Just think of it! (Jesus, you should have heard her.) Day in and day out she'd worked her fingers to the bone at that fag-packing machine, coming home at night dead to the wide yet cooking his dinners and mending his britches and cleaning his room out—it didn't bear thinking about. And now what had he gone and done, by way of thanks? (Robbed her purse? I asked myself quickly in the breathless interval; pawned the sheets and got drunk on the dough, drowned the cat, cut her window plants down with a pair of scissors?) No, he'd come home and told her he was getting married, just like that. It wasn't the getting married she minded—oh no, not that at all, of course it wasn't, because every young chap had to get married one day—so much as him not having brought the girl home before now for her to see and talk to. Why hadn't he done this? Was he ashamed of his mother? Didn't he think she was respectable enough to be seen by his young woman? Didn't he like to bring her back to his own home—you should have heard the way she said ' home ': it made my blood run cold—even though it was cleaned every day from top to bottom? Was he ashamed of his house as well? Or was it the young woman he was ashamed of? Was she *that* sort? Well, it was a mystery, it was and all. And what's more it wasn't fair, it wasn't. Do you think it's fair, Jim? Do you? Ay, maybe you do, but I don't, and I can't think of anybody else as would either.

She stopped shouting and thumping the table for a minute, and then the waterworks began. Fair would you say it was— she sobbed her socks off—after all I've struggled and sweated, getting you up for school every morning when you was little and sitting you down to porridge and bacon before you went out into the snow with your topcoat on, which was more than any of the other little rag-bags in the yard wore because their dads and mams boozed the dole money—(she said this, she

really did, because I was listening from a place where I couldn't
help but hear it—and I'll swear blind our dad never boozed a
penny of his dole money and we were still clambed half to
death on it. . .) And I think of all the times when you was
badly and I fetched the doctor, she went on screaming. Think
of it. But I suppose you're too self-pinnyated to think, which
is what my spoiling's done for you, aren't you? Eh?

The tears stopped. I think you might have had the common
decency to tell me you wanted to get married and had started
courting. She didn't know how he'd managed it, that she
didn't, especially when she'd kept her eyes on him so well. I
shouldn't have let you go twice a week to that Co-op youth
club of yourn, she shouted, suddenly realizing where he'd
seen his chance. That was it. By God it was, that was it. And
you telling me you was playing draughts and listening to
blokes talk politics! Politics! That's what they called it, was
it? First thing I knew. They called it summat else in my day,
and it worn't such a pretty name, either. Ay, by God. And
now you've got the cheek to stand there, still with your coat
on, not even offering to drop all this married business. (She
hadn't given him the chance to.) Why, Jim, how could you
think about getting married (tap on again) when I've been so
good to you? My poor lad, hasn't even realized what it's cost
me and how I've worked to keep us together all these years,
ever since your poor dad died. But I'll tell you one thing, my
lad (tap off, sharp, and the big finger wagging), you'd better
bring her to me and let me see her, and if she ain't up to
much, yer can let her go and look for somebody else, if she
still feels inclined.

By God, I was all of a tremble myself when I climbed down
from my perch, though I wouldn't have took it like Jim did,

but would have bashed her between the eyes and slung my hook there and then. Jim was earning good money and could have gone anywhere in the country, the bloody fool.

I suppose you'll be wondering how everybody in the yard knew all about what went on in Jim's house that night, and how it is that I'm able to tell word for word what Jim's mam said to him. Well, this is how it was: with Jim's house being so near the factory there's a ledge between the factory roof and his scullery window, the thickness of a double-brick wall, and I was thin-rapped enough to squeeze myself along this and listen-in. The scullery window was open, and so was the scullery door that led to the kitchen, so I heard all as went on. And nobody in the house twigged it either. I found this place out when I was eight, when I used to go monkey-climbing all over the buildings in our yard. It'd 'ave been dead easy to burgle the Scarfedales' house, except that there worn't anything much worth pinching, and except that the coppers would have jumped on me for it right away.

Well, we all knew then what went off right enough, but what surprised everybody was that Jim Scarfedale meant what he said and wasn't going to let his mam play the bully and stop him from getting married. I was on my perch the second night when sucky Jim brought his young woman to face his tub-thumping mother. She'd made him promise that much, at least.

I don't know why, but everybody in the yard expected to see some poor crumby-faced boss-eyed tart from Basford, a scruffy, half-baked, daft sort of piece that wouldn't say boo to a goose. But they got a shock. And so did I when I spied her through the scullery window. (Mrs. Scarfedale was crackers about fresh air, I will say that for her.) I'd never heard anybody talk so posh, as if she'd come straight out of an office, and it made me think that Jim hadn't lied after all when he said they'd talked about politics at the club.

"Good evening, Mrs. Scarfedale," she said as she came in. There was a glint in her eye, and a way she had, that made me think she'd been born talking as posh as she did. I wondered what she saw in Jim, whether she'd found out, unbeknown to any of us, that he'd been left some money, or was going to win the Irish Sweepstake. But no, Jim wasn't lucky enough for either, and I suppose his mam was thinking this at the same time as I was. Nobody shook hands.

"Sit down," Jim's mam said. She turned to the girl, and looked at her properly for the first time, hard. "I hear as you're wanting to marry my lad?"

"That's right, Mrs. Scarfedale," she said, taking the best chair, though sitting in it stiff and not at her ease. "We're going to be married quite soon." Then she tried to be more friendly, because Jim had given her the eye, like a little dog. "My name's Phyllis Blunt. Call me Phyllis." She looked at Jim, and Jim smiled at her because she was so nice to his mam after all. He went on smiling, as if he'd been practising all the afternoon in the lavatory mirror at the place where he worked. Phyllis smiled back, as though she'd been used to smiling like that all her life. Smiles all over the place, but it didn't mean a thing.

"What we have to do first," Jim said, putting his foot in it, though in a nice sociable way, "is get a ring."

I could see the way things were going right enough. His mam suddenly went blue in the face. "It ain't like *that*?" she brought out. "Is it?"

She couldn't touch Phyllis with a barge-pole. "I'm not pregnant, if that's what you mean."

Mrs. Scarfedale didn't know I was chiking, but I'll bet we

both thought together: Where's the catch in it, then? though it soon dawned on me that there wasn't any catch, at least not of the sort we must have thought of. And if this had dawned on Mrs. Scarfedale at the same time as it did on me there wouldn't have been the bigger argument that night— all of them going at it worse than tigers—and perhaps poor Jim wouldn't have got married as quick as he did.

"Well," his mother complained to our mam one day at the end of the yard about a month after they'd got spliced, "he's made his bed, and he can lie on it, even though it turns out to be a bed of nettles, which I for one told him it was bound to be."

Yet everybody hoped Jim would be able to keep on lying on it, because they'd always had something against such domineering strugglers as Mrs. Scarfedale. Not that everybody in our yard hadn't been a struggler—and still was—one way or another. You had to be, or just lay down and die. But Jim's mam sort of carried a placard about saying: I'm a struggler but a cut above everybody else because I'm so good at it. You could tell a mile off that she was a struggler and that was what nobody liked.

She was right about her lad though. Sod it, some people said. Jim didn't lie on his bed for long, though his wife wasn't a bad-looking piece and I can see now that he should have stayed between those sheets for longer than he did. Inside six months he was back, and we all wondered what could have gone wrong—as we saw him walking down the yard carrying a suit-case and two paper bundles, looking as miserable as sin and wearing the good suit he'd got married in to save it getting creased in the case. Well, I said to myself, I'll be back on my perch soon to find out what happened between Jim and

his posh missis. Yes, we'd all been expecting him to come back
to his mam if you want to know the dead honest truth, even
though we *hoped* he wouldn't, poor lad. Because in the first
three months of his being married he'd hardly come to see
her at all, and most people thought from this that he'd settled
down a treat and that married life must be suiting him. But I
knew different, for when a bloke's just got married he comes
home often to see his mam and dad—if he's happy. That's
only natural. But Jim stayed away, or tried to, and that showed
me that his wife was helping all she could to stop him seeing
his mam. After them first three months though he came home
more and more often—instead of the other way round—sometimes sleeping a night, which meant that his fights with
Phyllis was getting worse and worse. That last time he came
he had a bandage round his napper, a trilby hat stuck on top
like a lop-sided crown.

I got to my perch before Jim opened his back door, and I
was able to see him come in and make out what sort of a
welcome his mam gave him. She was clever, I will say that for
her. If she had thought about it she could have stopped his
marriage a dozen times by using a bit of craft I'll bet. There
was no: "I told you so. You should have listened to me and
then everything wouldn't have happened." No, she kissed him
and mashed him a cup of tea, because she knew that if she
played her cards right she could have him at home for good.
You could see how glad she was—could hardly stop herself
smiling—as she picked up his case and parcels and carried
them upstairs to his room, meaning to make his bed while the
kettle boiled, leaving him a blank ten-minute sit-down in peace
which she knew was just what he wanted.

But you should have seen poor old Jim, his face wicked-
badly, forty-five if he looked a day, as if he'd just been let out

of a Jap prisoner-of-war camp and staring—like he was crackers—at the same patch of carpet he'd stared at when he was only a kid on his pot. He'd always had a bit of a pain screwed into his mug—born that way I should think—but now it seemed as though he'd got an invisible sledgehammer hanging all the time in front of his miserable clock ready to fall against his snout. It would have made my heart bleed if I hadn't guessed he'd been such a sodding fool, getting wed with a nice tart and then making a mess of it all.

He sat like that for a quarter of an hour, and I'll swear blind he didn't hear a single one of the homely sounds coming from upstairs, of his mam making his bed and fixing up his room, like I did. And I kept wishing she'd make haste and get done with it, but she knew what she was doing all right, dusting the mirror and polishing the pictures for her sucky lad.

Well, she came down all of a smile (trying to hide it as best she could though) and set his bread and cheese out on the table, but he didn't touch a bite, only swigged three mugs of tea straight off while she sat in her chair and looked at him as if she, anyway, would make a good supper for him.

"I'll tell you, mam," he began as soon as she came and set herself staring at him from the other end of the table to get him blabbing just like this. "I've been through hell in the last six months, and I never want to go through it again."

It was like a dam breaking down. In fact the crack in a dam wall that you see on the pictures came into his forehead just like that, exactly. And once he got started there was no holding him back. "Tell me about it then, my lad"—though there was no need for her to have said this: he was trembling like a jelly, so that I was sometimes hard put to it to know what was going on. Honest, I can't tell it all in Jim's own

words because it'd break my heart; and I really did feel sorry
for him as he went on and on.

"Mam," he moaned, dipping bread and butter in his tea,
a thing I'm sure he'd never been able to do with his posh
missis at the table, "she led me a dog's life. In fact a dog
would have been better off in his kennel with an old bone to
chew now and again than I was with her. It was all right at
first, because you see, mam, she had some idea that a working
bloke like myself was good and honest and all that sort of
thing. I never knew whether she'd read this in a book or
whether she'd known working blokes before that were different from me, but she might have read it because she had a
few books in the house that I never looked at, and she never
mentioned any other blokes in her life. She used to say that it
was a treat to be able to marry and live with a bloke like me
who used his bare hands for a living, because there weren't
many blokes in the world, when you considered it, who did
good hard labouring work. She said she'd die if ever she
married a bloke as worked in an office and who crawled around
his boss because he wanted to get on. So I thought it would
go off all right, mam, honest I did, when she said nice things
like this to me. It made the netting factory look better to me,
and I didn't so much mind carrying bobbins from one machine
to another. I was happy with her and I thought that she was
happy with me. At first she made a bigger fuss of me than
before we were married even, and when I came home at night
she used to talk about politics and books and things, saying
how the world was made for blokes like me and that we
should run the world and not leave it to a lot of money-
grubbing capitalist bastards who didn't know any more about
it than to talk like babies week after week and get nothing
done that was any good to anybody.

"But to tell you the truth, mam, I was too tired to talk politics after I'd done a hard day's graft, and then she started to ask questions, and would get ratty after a while when she began to see that I couldn't answer what she wanted to know. She asked me all sorts of things, about my bringing up, about my dad, about all the neighbours in the terrace, but I could never tell her much, anyway, not what she wanted to know, and that started a bit of trouble. At first she packed my lunches and dinners and there was always a nice hot tea and some clothes to change into waiting for me when I came home, but later on she wanted me to have a bath every night, and that caused a bit of trouble because I was too tired to have a bath and often I was too fagged out even to change my clothes. I wanted to sit in my overalls listening to the wireless and reading the paper in peace. Once when I was reading the paper and she was getting mad because I couldn't get my eyes off the football results she put a match to the bottom of the paper and I didn't know about it till the flames almost came into my face. I got a fright, I can tell you, because I thought we were still happy then. And she made a joke about it, and even went out to buy me another newspaper, so I thought it was all right and that it was only a rum joke she'd played. But not long after that when I'd got the racing on the wireless she said she couldn't stand the noise and that I should listen to something better, so she pulled the plug out and wouldn't put it back.

"Yes, she did very well by me at first, that I will say, just like you, mam, but then she grew tired of it all, and started to read books all day, and there'd be nowt on the table at tea time when I came home dead to the wide except a packet of fags and a bag of toffees. She was all loving to me at first, but then she got sarcastic and said she couldn't stand the sight of

me. 'Here comes the noble savage,' she called out when I
came home, and used longer words I didn't know the meaning
of when I asked her where my tea was. 'Get it yourself,' she
said, and one day when I picked up one of her toffees from
the table she threw the poker at me. I said I was hungry, but
she just told me: 'Well, if you are, then crawl under the
table to me and I'll give you something.' Honest, mam, I can't
tell you one half of what went on, because you wouldn't want
to hear it."

(Not much, I thought. I could see her as large as life licking
her chops.)

"Tell me it all, my lad," she said. "Get it off your chest. I
can see you've had a lot to put up with."

"I did and all," he said. "The names she called me, mam.
It made my hair stand on end. I never thought she was that
sort, but I soon found out. She used to sit in front of the fire
with nothing on, and when I said that she should get dressed
in case a neighbour knocked at the door, she said she was
only warming her meal-ticket that the noble savage had given
her, and then she'd laugh, mam, in a way that made me so's
I couldn't move. I had to get out when she carried on like that
because I knew that if I stayed in she'd throw something and
do damage.

"I don't know where she is now. She packed up and took
her things, saying she never wanted to see me again, that I
could chuck myself in the canal for all she cared. She used to
shout a lot about going down to London and seeing some real
life, so I suppose that's where she's gone. There was four
pounds ten and threepence in a jam-jar on the kitchen shelf
and when she'd gone that was gone as well.

"So I don't know, our mam, about anything, or what I'm
going to do. I'd like to live here again with you if you'll have

me. I'll pay you two quid a week regular for my board, and see you right. I can't put up with any of that any more because I can't stand it, and I don't suppose I'll ever leave home again after all that little lot of trouble. So if you'll have me back, mam, I'll be ever so glad. I'll work hard for you, that I will, and you'll never have to worry again. I'll do right by you and pay you back a bit for all the struggle you had in bringing me up. I heard at work the other day as I'm to have a ten bob rise next week, so if you let me stay I'll get a new wireless and pay the deposit on it. So let me stay, our mam, because, I tell you, I've suffered a lot."

And the way she kissed him made me sick, so I got down from my monkey-perch.

Jim Scarfedale stayed, right enough, the great big baby. He was never happier in his life after getting the O.K. from his old woman. All his worries were over, he'd swear blind they were, even if you tried to tell him what a daft sod he was for not packing his shaving tackle and getting out, which I did try to tell him, only he thought I was cracked even more than he was himself, I suppose. His mother thought she'd got him back for good, though, and so did we all, but we were off the mark by a mile. If you weren't stone-blind you could see he was never the same old Jim after he'd been married: he got broody and never spoke to a soul, and nobody, not even his mam, could ever get out of him where he went to every night. His face went pudgy-white and his sandy mouse-hair fell out so much that he was nearly bald in six months. Even the few freckles he had went pale. He used to slink back from wherever he'd been at twelve o'clock, whether the night was winter or summer, and never a bloke would know what he got up to. And if you asked him right out loud, like as if you were cracking a bit of a joke: "Where you been, Jim?" he'd make as if he hadn't heard a sound.

It must have been a couple of years later when the copper came up our yard one moonlight night: I saw him from my bedroom window. He turned the corner, and I dodged back before he could spot me. You're in for it now, I said to myself, ripping lead from that empty house on Buckingham Street. You should have had more sense, you daft bogger (frightened to death I was, though I don't know why now), especially when you only got three and a tanner for it from Cooky. I always said you'd end up in Borstal, and here comes the copper to get you.

Even when he went on past our house I thought it was only because he'd got mixed up in the numbers and that he'd swing back at any minute. But no, it was the Scarfedales' door he wanted, and I'd never known a happier feeling than when I heard that rap-rap-rapping and knew that this time they hadn't come for me. Never again, I sang to myself, never again—so happy that I got the stitch—they can keep their bleeding lead.

Jim's mam screamed as soon as the copper mentioned her name. Even from where I was I heard her say: "He's never gone and got run over, has he?"

Then I could hear no more, but a minute later she walked up the yard with the copper, and I saw her phizzog by the lamplight, looking set hard like granite, as if she would fall down and kick the bucket if you as much as whispered a word to her. The copper had to hold her arm.

It all came out next morning—the queerest case the yard had ever known. Blokes had been put inside for burglary, deserting, setting fire to buildings, bad language, being blind drunk, grabbing hold of grown women and trying to give them what-for, not paying maintenance money, running up big debts for wirelesses and washing machines and then selling them, poaching, trespassing, driving off in cars that didn't belong to them, trying to commit suicide, attempted murder, assault and battery, snatching handbags, shoplifting, fraud, forgery, pilfering from work, bashing each other about, and all sorts of larks that didn't mean much. But Jim did something I hadn't heard about before, at least not in our yard.

He'd been at it for months as well, taking a bus four miles across town to places where nobody knew him and waiting in old dark streets near some lit-up beer-off for little girls of ten and eleven to come walking along carrying jugs to get their dads a pint in. And sucky Jim would jump out of his hiding place near pieces of waste-ground and frighten the life out of them and get up to his dirty tricks. I can't understand why he did it, I can't, I really can't, but did it he did, and got copped for it as well. He did it so often that somebody must have sprung a trap, because one hard-luck night they collared him and he was put inside for eighteen months. You should have heard the telling-off he got from the judge. I'll bet the poor sod didn't know where to put his face, though I'm sure there's many a judge that's done the same, if not worse, than Jim. "We've got to put you in clink," the judge said, "not only for the good of little girls but for your own good as well. People have got to be protected from the likes of you, you dirty sod."

After that we never saw him again in our yard, because by the time he came out his mother had got a house and a new job in Derby, so's they could settle down where nobody knew them I suppose. Jim was the only bloke in our yard that ever got a big spread in *all* the newspapers, as far as I can remember, and nobody would have thought he had it in him, though

I think it was a bit like cheating, getting in on them with a thing like that.

Which is why I think nobody should hang on to his mother's apron strings for such a long time like Jim did, or they might go the same way. And that's why I look at that atlas under my desk at school instead of doing sums (up through Derbyshire and into Manchester, then up to Glasgow, across to Edinburgh, and down again to London, saying hello to mam and dad on the way) because I hate doing sums, especially when I think I can already reckon up all the money I'm ever likely to scoop from any small-time gas-meter.

The Decline and Fall of Frankie Buller

SITTING in what has come to be called my study, a room in the first-floor flat of a ramshackle Majorcan house, my eyes move over racks of books around me. Row after row of coloured backs and dusty tops, they give an air of distinction not only to the room but to the whole flat, and one can sense the thoughts of occasional visitors who stoop down discreetly during drinks to read their titles:

"A Greek lexicon, Homer in the original. He knows Greek! (Wrong, those books belong to my brother-in-law.) Shakespeare, The Golden Bough, a Holy Bible bookmarked with tapes and paper. He even reads it! Euripides and the rest, and a dozen mouldering Baedekers. What a funny idea to collect them! Proust, all twelve volumes! I never could wade through that lot. (Neither did I.) Dostoevsky. My God, is *he* still going strong?"

And so on and so on, items that have become part of me, foliage that has grown to conceal the bare stem of my real personality, what I was like before I ever saw these books, or any book at all, come to that. Often I would like to rip them away from me one by one, extract their shadows out of my mouth and heart, cut them neatly with a scalpel from my jungle-brain. Impossible. You can't wind back the clock that sits grinning on the marble shelf. You can't even smash its face in and forget it.

Yesterday we visited the house of a friend who lives further along the valley, away from the town noises so that sitting on the terrace with eyes half-closed and my head leaning back in a deck-chair, beneath a tree of half-ripe medlars and with the smell of plundered oranges still on my hands, I heard the sound of a cuckoo coming from the pine woods on the mountain slopes.

The cuckoo accomplished what a surgeon's knife could not. I was plunged back deep through the years into my natural state, without books and without the knowledge that I am supposed to have gained from them. I was suddenly landed beyond all immediate horizons of the past by the soft, sharp, fluting whistle of the cuckoo, and set down once more within the kingdom of Frankie Buller.

We were marching to war, and I was part of his army, with an elderberry stick at the slope and my pockets heavy with smooth, flat, well-chosen stones that would skim softly and swiftly through the air, and strike the foreheads of enemies. My plimsoll shoes were sprouting bunions, and there must have been a patch at the back of my trousers and holes in my socks, because I can never remember a time when there weren't, up to the age of fourteen.

The roll-call revealed eleven of us, yet Frankie was a full-blown centurion with his six-foot spear-headed railing at the slope, and his rusty dustbin lid for a shield. To make our numbers look huge to an enemy he marched us down from the bridge and across the field in twos, for Frankie was a good tactician, having led the local armies since he was fifteen years old.

At that time his age must have stood between twenty and twenty-five. Nobody seemed to know for sure, Frankie least of all, and it was supposed that his parents found it politic to keep the secret closely. When we asked Frankie how old he was he answered with the highly improbable number of: "'Undred an' fifty-eight." This reply was logically followed by another question: "When did you leave school, then?" Sometimes he would retort scornfully to this: "I never went to school." Or he might answer with a proud grin: "I didn't leave, I ran away."

I wore short trousers, and he wore long trousers, so it was impossible for me to say how tall he was in feet and inches. In appearance he seemed like a giant. He had grey eyes and dark hair, and regular features that would have made him passably handsome had not a subtle air of pre-pubescent unreliability lurked in his eyes and around the lines of his low brow. In body and strength he lacked nothing for a full-grown man.

We in the ranks automatically gave him the title of General, but he insisted on being addressed as Sergeant-Major, because his father had been a sergeant-major in the First World War. "My dad was wounded in the war," he told us every time we saw him. "He got a medal and shell-shock, and because he got shell-shock, that's why I'm like I am."

He was glad and proud of being 'like he was' because it meant he did not have to work in a factory all day and earn his living like other men of his age. He preferred to lead the gang of twelve-year-olds in our street to war against the same age group of another district. Our street was a straggling line of ancient back-to-backs on the city's edge, while the enemy district was a new housing estate of three long streets which had outflanked us and left us a mere pocket of country in which to run wild—a few fields and allotment gardens, which was reason enough for holding an eternal grudge against them. People from the slums in the city-centre lived in the housing estate, so that our enemies were no less ferocious than we, except that they didn't have a twenty-year-old backward youth like Frankie to lead them into battle. The inhabitants of the housing estate had not discarded their slum habits, so that the area became known to our street as 'Sodom'.

"We're gooin' ter raid Sodom today," Frankie said, when we were lined-up on parade. He did not know the Biblical association of the word, thinking it a name officially given by the city council.

So we walked down the street in twos and threes, and formed up on the bridge over the River Lean. Frankie would order us to surround any stray children we met with on the way, and if they wouldn't willingly fall in with us as recruits he would follow one of three courses. First: he might have them bound with a piece of clothes-line and brought with us by force; second: threaten to torture them until they agreed to come with us of their own free will; third: bat them across the head with his formidable hand and send them home weeping, or snarling back curses at him from a safe distance. I had come to join his gang through clause number two, and had stayed with it for profitable reasons of fun and adventure. My father often said: "If I see yo' gooin' about wi' that daft Frankie Buller I'll clink yer tab-'ole."

Although Frankie was often in trouble with the police he could never, even disregarding his age, be accurately described as a 'juvenile delinquent'. He was threatened regularly by the law with being sent to Borstal, but his antics did not claim for him a higher categorical glory than that of 'general nuisance' and so kept him out of the clutches of such institutions. His father drew a pension due to wounds from the war, and his mother worked at the tobacco factory, and on this combined income the three of them seemed to live at a higher standard than the rest of us, whose fathers were permanent appendages at the dole office. The fact that Frankie was an only child in a district where some families numbered up to half a dozen was accounted for by the rumour that the father, having seen Frankie at birth, had decided to run no more risks. Another whispered reason concerned the nature of Mr. Buller's pensionable wound.

We used to ask Frankie, when we made camp in the woods and squatted around a fire roasting plundered potatoes after victory, what he was going to do when the Second War started.

"Join up," he would say, non-committally.

"What in, Frankie?" someone would ask respectfully, for Frankie's age and strength counted for much more than the fact that the rest of us knew roughly how to read and write.

Frankie responded by hurling a piece of wood at his inter-rogator. He was a crackshot at any kind of throw, and rarely missed hitting the shoulder or chest. "Yer've got to call me 'SIR'!" he roared, his arms trembling with rightful anger. "Yer can get out to the edge of the wood and keep guard for that." The bruised culprit slunk off through the bushes, clutching his pole and stones.

"What would you join, sir?" a more knowing ranker said.

Such respect made him amiable:

"The Sherwood Foresters. That's the regiment my dad was in. He got a medal in France for killin' sixty-three Jerries in one day. He was in a dug-out, see"—Frankie could act this with powerful realism since seeing *All Quiet on the Western Front* and *The Lives of a Bengal Lancer*—"behind his machine gun, and the Jerries come over at dawn, and my dad seed 'em and started shootin'. They kept comin' over, but the Old Man just kept on firin' away—der-der-der-der-der-der-der—even when all his pals was dead. My Old Man was 'it with a bullet as well, but 'e din't let go of 'is gun, and the Jerries was fallin' dead like flies, dropping all round 'im, and when the rest o' the Sherwoods come back to 'elp 'im and stop the Jerries coming over, 'e counted sixty-three dead bodies in front on 'is gun. So they gen 'im a medal and sent 'im back ter England."

He looked around at the semicircle of us. "What do yer think o' that, then?" he demanded savagely, as if he himself were the hero and we were disputing it. "All right," he ordered, when we had given the required appreciation to his father's exploits, "I want yer all ter scout round for wood so's the fire wain't goo out."

Frankie was passionately interested in war. He would often slip a penny into my hand and tell me to fetch an *Evening Post* so that I could read to him the latest war news from China, Abyssinia, or Spain, and he would lean against the wall of his house, his grey eyes gazing at the roofs across the street, saying whenever I stopped for breath: "Go on, Alan, read me a bit more. Read me that bit about Madrid again. . . ."

Frankie was a colossus, yet a brave man who formed us up and laid us in the hollows of a field facing the railway embankment that defended the approaches to the streets of Sodom. We would wait for an hour, a dozen of us with faces pressed to the earth, feeling our sticks and trying to stop the stones in our pockets from rattling. If anyone stirred Frankie would whisper out a threat: "The next man to move, I'll smash 'im with my knobkerrie."

We were three hundred yards from the embankment. The grass beneath us was smooth and sweet, and Frankie chewed it by the mouthful, stipulating that no one else must do so because it was worse than Deadly Nightshade. It would kill us in five second flat if we were to eat it, he went on, but it would do him no harm because he was proof against poison of all kinds. There was magic inside him that would not let it kill him; he was a witch doctor, and, for anyone who wasn't, the grass would scorch his guts away.

An express train came out of the station, gathered speed on the bend, and blocked the pink eavings of Sodom from view while we lifted our heads from the grass and counted the carriages. Then we saw our enemies, several figures standing on the railway tracks, brandishing sticks and throwing stones with playful viciousness into a pool of water down the slope.

"It's the Sodom gang," we whispered.

"Keep quiet," Frankie hissed. "How many do you see? "

"Can't tell."

"Eight."

"There's more comin' up."

"Pretend they're Germans," Frankie said.

They came down the slope and, one by one, lifted themselves over to our side of the railings. On the embankment they shouted and called out to each other, but once in the field they walked close together without making much noise. I saw nine of them, with several more still boldly trespassing on the railway line. I remembered that we were eleven, and while waiting for the signal to rush forward I kept saying to myself: "It won't be long now. It can't be long now."

Frankie mumbled his final orders. "You lot go left. You other lot go right. We'll go in front. I want 'em surrounded." The only military triumph he recognized was to surround and capture.

He was on his feet, brandishing an iron spear and waving a shield. We stood up with him and, stretched out in a line, advanced slowly, throwing stones as fast as our arms would move into the concentric ring of the enemy gang.

It was a typical skirmish. Having no David to bring against

our Goliath they slung a few ineffectual stones and ran back helter-skelter over the railings, mounting the slope to the railway line. Several of them were hit.

" Prisoners! " Frankie bellowed, but they bolted at the last moment and escaped. For some minutes stones flew between field and embankment, and our flanks were unable to push forward and surround. The enemy exulted then from the railway line because they had a harvest of specially laid stones between the tracks, while we had grass underfoot, with no prospect of finding more ammunition when our pockets were emptied. If they rallied and came back at us, we would have to retreat half a mile before finding stones at the bridge.

Frankie realized all this in a second. The same tactical situation had occurred before. Now some of us were hit. A few fell back. Someone's eye was cut. My head was streaming with blood, but I disregarded this for the moment because I was more afraid of the good hiding I would catch from my father's meaty fist at home for getting into a fight, than blood and a little pain. ("Yer've bin wi' that Frankie Buller agen, ain't yer? " Bump. "What did I tell yer? Not ter ger wi' 'im, din't I? " Bump. "And yer don't do what I tell yer, do you? " Bump. "Yer'll keep on gooin' wi' that Frankie Buller tell yer as daft as 'e is, wain't yer? " Bump-bump.)

We were wavering. My pockets were light and almost empty of stones. My arms ached with flinging them.

" All right if we charge, lads? " Frankie called out.

There was only one answer to his words. We were with him, right into the ovens of a furnace had he asked it. Perhaps he led us into these bad situations, in which no retreat was possible, just for the fine feeling of a glorious win or lose.

" Yes! " we all shouted together.

" Come on, then," he bawled out at the top of his voice:

"CHARGE!"

His great strides carried him the hundred yards in a few seconds, and he was already climbing the railing. Stones from the Sodom lot were clanging and rattling against his shield. Lacking the emblematic spear and dustbin lid of a leader we went forward more slowly, aiming our last stones at the gang on the embankment above.

As we mounted the railings on his left and right Frankie was half-way up the slope, within a few yards of the enemy. He exhorted his wings all the time to make more speed and surround them, waving his dangerous spear-headed length of iron now before their faces. From lagging slightly we suddenly swept in on both flanks, reaching the railway line in one rush to replenish our stocks of ammunition, while Frankie went on belabouring them from the front.

They broke, and ran down the other slope, down into the streets of Sodom, scattering into the refuge of their rows of pink houses whose doors were already scratched and scarred, and where, it was rumoured, they kept coal in their bathrooms (though this was secretly envied by us as a commodious coal-scuttle so conveniently near to the kitchen) and strung poaching nets out in their back gardens.

When the women of our street could think of no more bad names to call Frankie Buller for leading their children into fights that resulted in black eyes, torn clothes, and split heads, they called him a Zulu, a label that Frankie nevertheless came to accept as a tribute, regarding it as being synonymous with bravery and recklessness. "Why do you run around with that bleddy Zulu?" a mother demanded from her child as she tore up one of father's old shirts for a bandage or patch. And immediately there was conjured up before you Frankie, a wild figure wielding spear and dustbin lid, jumping up and down before leading his gang into battle. When prisoners were taken he would have them tied to a tree or fence-post, then order his gang to do a war dance around them. After the performance, in which he in his fierce panoply sometimes took part, he would have a fire built near by and shout out that he was going to have the prisoners tortured to death now. He once came so near to carrying out this threat that one of us ran back and persuaded Frankie's father to come and deal with his son and set the prisoners free. And so Mr. Buller and two other men, one of them my father, came striding down the steps of the bridge. They walked quickly across the field, short, stocky, black-browed Chris, and bald Buller with his walrus moustache. But the same person who had given the alarm crept back into Frankie's camp and gave warning there, so that when the three men arrived, ready to buckle Frankie down and drive him home, they found nothing except a kicked-out fire and a frightened but unharmed pair of captives still tied to a tree.

It was a fact that Frankie's acts of terrorism multiplied as the war drew nearer, though many of them passed unnoticed because of the preoccupied and brooding atmosphere of that summer. He would lead his gang into allotments and break into the huts, scattering tools and flower seeds with a maniacal energy around the garden, driving a lawnmower over lettuce-heads and parsley, leaving a litter of decapitated chrysanthemums in his track. His favourite sport was to stand outside one of the huts and throw his spear at it with such force that its iron barb ran right through the thin wood.

We had long since said farewell to the novelty of possessing gasmasks. Frankie led us on a foray over the fields one day, out on a raid with masks on our faces—having sworn that the white cloud above the wood was filled with mustard gas let loose from the Jerry trenches on the other side—and they became so broken up in the scuffle that we threw each one ceremoniously into a fire before going home, preferring to say we had lost them rather than show the tattered relics that remained.

So many windows were broken, dustbins upturned, air let out of bicycle tyres, and heads split as a result of pyrrhic victories in gang raids—for he seemed suddenly to be losing his military genius—that it became dangerous for Frankie to walk down our street. Stuffing a few shreds of tobacco into one of his father's old pipes—tobacco that we collected for him as cigarette-ends—he would walk along the middle of the street, and suddenly an irate woman would rush out of an entry wielding a clothes-prop and start frantically hitting him.

"I saw you empty my dustbin last night, you bleddy Zulu, you grett daft baby. Take that, and that, and that!"

"It worn't me, missis. I swear to God it worn't," he would shout in protest, arms folded over his head and galloping away to avoid her blows.

"Yo' come near my house agen," she shouted after him, "and I'll cool yer down wi' a bucket o' water, yo' see'f I don't."

Out of range, he looked back at her, bewildered, angry, his blood boiling with resentment. He shouted out the worst swear-words he knew, and disappeared into his house, slamming the door behind him.

It was not only the outbreak of the war that caused Frankie's downfall. Partly it came about because there was a romantic side to his nature that evinced itself in other means than mock warfare. At the end of many afternoons in the summer he stood at the top of our street and waited for the girls to come out of the tobacco factory. Two thousand worked there, and about a quarter of them passed by every evening on their way home to tea.

He mostly stood there alone in his black corduroy trousers, patched jacket, and a collarless shirt belonging to his father, but if an older member of the gang stayed for company it by no means inhibited his particular brand of courtship. He had the loudest mouth-whistle in the street, and this was put to good and musical use as the girls went by with arms linked in twos and threes.

"Hey up, duck!" he would call out. "How are yer?"

A shrug of the shoulders, a toss of the head, laughter, or a sharp retort came back.

"Can I tek yer out tonight?" he cried with a loud laugh. "Do you want me to treat you to't pictures?"

Occasionally a girl would cross to the other side of the road to avoid him, and she would be singled out for his most special witticism:

"Hey up, good-lookin', can I cum up and see yer some time?"

Responses flew back like this, laced around with much laughter:

"It'll cost yer five quid!"

"Ye'r daft, me duck, yer foller balloons!"

"I'll meet you at the Grand at eight. Don't forget to be there, because I shall!"

It was his greatest hour of mature diversion. He was merely acting his age, following, though in a much exaggerated manner, what the other twenty-year-olds did in the district. The consummation of these unique courtships took place among the bulrushes, in the marsh between the River Lean and the railway line where Frankie rarely led his gang. He stalked alone (a whistled-at girl accompanying him only as a dim picture in his mind) along concealed paths to catch tadpoles, and then to lie by himself in a secret place where no one could see him, self-styled boss of osiers, elderberry and bordering oak. From which journey he returned pale and shifty-eyed with guilt and a pleasurable memory.

He stood at the street corner every evening as the summer wore on, at first with many of the gang, but later alone because his remarks to the passing factory girls were no longer innocent, so that one evening a policeman came and drove him away from the street corner for ever. During those same months hundreds of loaded lorries went day after day to the edge of the marsh and dumped rubble there, until Frankie's secret hiding place was obliterated, and above it lay the firm foundation for another branch of the tobacco factory.

On the Sunday morning that my mother and father shook their heads over Chamberlain's melancholy voice issuing from the webbed heart-shaped speaker of our wireless set, I met Frankie in the street.

I asked what he would do now there was a war on, for I assumed that in view of his conscriptable age he would be called-up with the rest of the world. He seemed inert and sad, and I took this to be because of the war, a mask of proper seriousness that should be on everybody's face, even though I didn't feel it to be on my own. I also noticed that when he spoke he did so with a stammer. He sat on the pavement with his back leaning against the wall of some house, instinctively knowing that no one would think of pummelling him with a clothes-prop today.

"I'll just wait for my calling-up papers," he answered. "Then I'll get in the Sherwood Foresters."

"If I get called-up I'll go in the navy," I put in, when he

did not offer an anecdote about his father's exploits in the last war.

"The army's the only thing to join, Alan," he said with deep conviction, standing up and taking out his pipe.

He suddenly smiled, his dejection gone. "I'll tell you what, after dinner we'll get the gang together and go over New Bridge for manœuvres. I've got to get you all into shape now there's a war on. We'll do a bit o' training. P'raps we'll meet some o' the Sodom lot."

As we marched along that afternoon Frankie outlined his plan for our future. When we were about sixteen, he said, if the war was still on—it was bound to be because the Germans were tough, his old man told him so, though they wouldn't win in the end because their officers always sent the men over the top first—he'd take us down to the recruiting depot in town and enlist us together, all at the same time. In that way he—Frankie—would be our platoon commander.

It was a wonderful idea. All hands were thrust into the air.

The field was clear over New Bridge. We stood in a line along the parapet and saw without comment the newest proof of the city's advance. The grazing lands and allotments were now cut off from the main spread of the countryside by a boulevard sprouting from Sodom's new houses, with cars and Corporation double-deckers already running along it.

There was no sign of the Sodom lot, so Frankie ordered three of us to disappear into the gullies and hollows for the rest of the gang to track down. The next item on the training programme was target practice, a tin can set on a tree trunk until it was knocked over with stones from fifty yards. After fencing lessons and wrestling matches six of the Sodom gang appeared on the railway line, and at the end of a quick brutal skirmish they were held fast as prisoners. Frankie wished neither to keep them nor harm them, and let them go after making them swear an oath of allegiance to the Sherwood Foresters.

At seven o'clock we were formed up in double file to be marched back. Someone grumbled that it was a late hour to get home to tea, and for once Frankie succumbed to what I clearly remembered seeing as insubordination. He listened to the complaint and decided to cut our journey short by leading us across the branch-line that ran into the colliery. The factories and squalid streets on the hill had turned a sombre ochred colour, as if a storm would burst during the night, and the clouds above the city were pink, giving an unreal impression of profound silence so that we felt exposed, as if the railwayman in the distant signal box could see us and hear every word we spoke.

One by one we climbed the wire fence, Frankie crouching in the bushes and telling us when he thought the path was clear. He sent us over one at a time, and we leapt the six tracks yet kept our backs bent, as if we were passing a machine-gun post. Between the last line and the fence stood an obstacle in the form of a grounded railway carriage that served as a repair and tool-storage shed. Frankie had assured us that no one was in it, but when we were all across, the others already rushing through the field and up on to the lane, I turned around and saw a railwayman come out of the door and stop Frankie just as he was making for the fence.

I didn't hear any distinct words, only the muffled sound of arguing. I kept down between the osiers and watched the railwayman poking his finger at Frankie's chest as if he were giving him some really strong advice. Then Frankie began to wave his hands in the air, as though he could not tolerate being stopped in this way, with his whole gang looking on from the field, as he thought.

Then, in one vivid second, I saw Frankie snatch a pint bottle from his jacket pocket and hit the railwayman over the head with it. In the exaggerated silence I heard the crash, and a cry of shock, rage, and pain from the man. Frankie then turned and ran in my direction, leaping like a zebra over the fence. When he drew level and saw me he cried wildly:

"Run, Alan, run. He asked for it. He asked for it."

And we ran.

The next day my brothers, sisters and myself were loaded into Corporation buses and transported to Worksop. We were evacuated, our few belongings thrust into paper carrier-bags, away from the expected bombs, along with most other children of the city. In one fatal blow Frankie's gang was taken away from him, and Frankie himself was carried off to the police station for hitting the railwayman on the head with a bottle. He was also charged with trespassing.

It may have been that the beginning of the war coincided with the end of Frankie's so-called adolescence, though ever after traces of it frequently appeared in his behaviour. For instance he would still tramp from one end of the city to the other, even through smokescreen and blackout, in the hope of finding some cinema that showed a good cowboy film.

I didn't meet Frankie again for two years. One day I saw a man pushing a handcart up the old street in which we did not live any more. The man was Frankie, and the handcart was loaded with bundles of wood, the sort of kindling that housewives spread over a crumpled-up *Evening Post* before making a morning fire. We couldn't find much to talk about, and Frankie seemed condescending in his attitude to me, as though ashamed to be seen talking to one so much younger than himself. This was not obvious in any plain way, yet I felt it and, being thirteen, resented it. Times had definitely altered. We just weren't pals any more. I tried to break once again into the atmosphere of old times by saying:

"Did you try to get into the army then, Frankie?"

I realize now that it was an indiscreet thing to say, and might have hurt him. I did not notice it then, yet I remembered his sensitivity as he answered:

"What do you mean? I *am* in the army. I joined-up a year ago. The old man's back in the army as well—sergeant-major —and I'm in 'is cumpny."

The conversation quickly ended. Frankie pushed his barrow to the next entry, and began unloading his bundles of wood.

I didn't meet him for more than ten years. In that time I too had done my 'sodjerin'', in Malaya, and I had forgotten the childish games we used to play with Frankie Buller, and the pitched battles with the Sodom lot over New Bridge.

I didn't live in the same city any more. I suppose it could be said that I had risen from the ranks. I had become a writer of sorts, having for some indescribable reason, after the evacuation and during the later bombs, taken to reading books.

I went back home to visit my family, and on my way through the streets about six o'clock one winter's evening, I heard someone call out:

"Alan!"

I recognized the voice instantly. I turned and saw Frankie standing before a cinema billboard, trying to read it. He was about thirty-five now, no longer the javelin-wielding colossus he once appeared, but nearer my own height, thinner, an unmistakable air of meekness in his face, almost respectable in his cap and black topcoat with white muffler tucked neatly inside. I noticed the green medal-ribbon on the lapel of his coat, and that confirmed what I had heard about him from time to time during the last ten years. From being the sergeant-major of our gang he had become a private soldier in the Home Guard, a runner indeed in his father's company. With tin-hat on his sweating low-browed head Frankie had stalked with messages through country whose every blade of grass he knew.

He was not my leader any more, and we both instantly recognized the fact as we shook hands. Frankie's one-man wood business had prospered, and he now went around the streets with a pony and cart. He wasn't well-off, but he was his own employer. The outspoken ambition of our class was to become one's own boss. He knew he wasn't the leader of kindred spirits any more, while he probably wondered as we spoke whether or not I might be, which could have accounted for his shyness.

Not only had we both grown up in our different ways since the days when with dustbin lid and railing-spear he led his battalion into pitiless stone-throwing forays, but something of which I did not know had happened to him. Coming from the same class and, one might say, from the same childhood, there should have been some tree-root of recognition between us, despite the fact that our outer foliage of leaves would have wilted somewhat before each other's differing shade and colour. But there was no contact and I, being possessed of what the world I had moved into often termed 'heightened consciousness', knew that it was due as much to something in Frankie as in me.

"'Ow are yer gooin' on these days, Frankie?" I asked,

revelling in the old accent, though knowing that I no longer had the right to use it.

His stammer was just short of what we would once have derisively called a stutter. "All right now. I feel a lot better, after that year I had in hospital."

I looked him quickly and discreetly up and down for evidence of a lame foot, a broken limb, a scar; for why else did people go to hospital? "What were you in for?" I asked.

In replying, his stammer increased. I felt he hesitated because for one moment he did not know which tone to take, though the final voice he used was almost proud, and certainly serious. "Shock treatment. That's why I went."

"What did they give you shock treatment for, Frankie?" I asked this question calmly, genuinely unable to comprehend what he told me, until the full horrible details of what Frankie must have undergone flashed into my mind. And then I wanted power in me to tear down those white-smocked mad interferers with Frankie's coal-forest world, wanted to wipe out their hate and presumption.

He pulled his coat collar up because, in the dusk, it was beginning to rain. "Well, you see, Alan," he began, with what I recognized now as a responsible and conforming face, "I had a fight with the Old Man, and after it I blacked out. I hurt my dad, and he sent for the police. They fetched a doctor, and the doctor said I'd have to go to the hospital." They had even taught him to call it 'hospital'. In the old days he would have roared with laughter and said:

"'Sylum!"

"I'm glad you're better now, then," I said, and during the long pause that followed I realized that Frankie's world was after all untouchable, that the conscientious-scientific-methodical probers could no doubt reach it, could drive it into hiding, could kill the physical body that housed it, but had no power in the long run really to harm such minds. There is a part of the jungle that the scalpel can never reach.

He wanted to go. The rain was worrying him. Then, remembering why he had called me over, he turned to face the broad black lettering on a yellow background. "Is that for the Savoy?" he asked, nodding at the poster.

"Yes," I said.

He explained apologetically: "I forgot me glasses, Alan. Can you read it for me, and tell me what's on tonight."

"Sure, Frankie." I read it out: "Gary Cooper, in *Saratoga Trunk*."

"I wonder if it's any good?" he asked. "Do you think it's a cowboy picture, or a love picture?"

I was able to help him on this point. I wondered, after the shock treatment, which of these subjects he would prefer. Into what circle of his dark, devil-populated world had the jolts of electricity penetrated? "I've seen that picture before," I told him. "It's a sort of cowboy picture. There's a terrific train smash at the end."

Then I saw. I think he was surprised that I shook his hand so firmly when we parted. My explanation of the picture's main points acted on him like a charm. Into his eyes came the same glint I had seen years ago when he stood up with spear and shield and roared out: "CHARGE!" and flung himself against showers of sticks and flying stones.

"It sounds good," he said. "That's the picture for me. I's'll see that."

He pulled his cap lower down, made sure that his coat-collar covered his throat and neck, and walked with stirred imagination off into the driving rain.

"Cheerio, Frank," I called out as he turned the corner. I

wondered what would be left of him by the time they had finished. Would they succeed in tapping and draining dry the immense subterranean reservoir of his dark inspired mind?

I watched him. He ignored the traffic-lights, walked diagonally across the wide wet road, then ran after a bus and leapt safely on to its empty platform.

And I with my books have not seen him since. It was like saying goodbye to a big part of me, for ever.

A Note about the Author

ALAN SILLITOE *was born in 1928 in Nottingham, England, and grew up in the slums of that industrial city. The son of a laborer in a tannery, he left school at fourteen to work in a bicycle plant, then in a plywood mill, and later in another factory, as a capstan-lathe operator. He was called up just after the war and spent two years as an R.A.F. radio operator in Malaya. After his discharge, he married an American girl and lived for several years on Majorca, where he met and became friends with the poet Robert Graves. In a few short years, with the publication of six books of fiction and one of non-fiction, Mr. Sillitoe has come to be regarded as one of the most important British writers of the postwar decades. His first novel,* Saturday Night and Sunday Morning, *was awarded the Authors' Club prize for the best English first novel of 1958. His second piece of fiction,* The Loneliness of the Long-distance Runner, *won the coveted Hawthornden Prize in 1959. He has also written* The General *(1961),* Key to the Door *(1962),* The Ragman's Daughter and Other Stories *(1964),* Road to Volgograd *(1964),* The Death of William Posters *(1965),* Tree on Fire *(1968) and* Love in the Environs of Voronezh and Other Poems *(1969).*

A NOTE ON THE TYPE

The Loneliness of the Long-distance Runner is set in 11-point JULIANA, 2 points leaded.

JULIANA is a new Linotype face of sixteenth-century Italian style, yet entirely original, designed by S. L. Hartz, an eminent Dutch typographer and engraver.

This book is among the first to have been printed in this type-face anywhere in the world.